Empty Nights

By

Jack Dowd

This is a work of fiction. Names, characters, businesses, places, events and incidents are either the products of the author's imagination or used in a fictitious manner. Any resemblance to actual persons, living or dead, or actual events and locations, are purely coincidental.

Empty Nights

Copyright © 2018 by MommaShark Press
All rights reserved. This book or any portion thereof may not be reproduced or used in any manner whatsoever without the express written permission of the author except for the use of brief quotations in a book review.

Editing by Katie Clem

Cover Design Copyright © 2018 by Hedvig R.Z Sjöström

First Printing 2018

ISBN 978-1-9164436-0-0

FIRST Edition

www.MommaSharkPress.com

MommaShark Press
P.O. Box 99
Kemah, TX 77565

Acknowledgements

This novel is dedicated to my mother and the rest of my family for supporting me in my writing career. I would also like to thank my lecturers and classmates at London South Bank University and my close friends at University College London. A special thanks to my editor Katie Clem, illustrator Hedvig R.Z Sjöström and my publishing group MommaShark Press without whom this book wouldn't be possible.

Wednesday 24 January, 20:11.

Milton's Mill factory

Doctor West suggested that I should write a blog to unpack everything and I need to tell you about my school trip.

'Does anyone recognise where we are?' Mr Roth asked.

We were on a patch of wasteland next to the River Thames. I could see the riverbank from my position at the back of the class. Dead bushes separated the land from the river and across the water were rows of warehouses. Weeds sprouted out from between the cracked concrete that pathed the ground. A Dockland's Light Railway train rattled above us on the elevated track and to our left was a factory, white smoke pouring out of its chimney. The ruins of the old factory lay before us, all that remained was a crumbling wall sprayed with graffiti and several stone pillars.

It was obviously the disused factory we had been talking about in our last geography lesson, but I didn't say anything. When no one, apart from the seagulls answered, Mr Roth said,

'This is the Milton's Mill Factory, or it was before it was torn down. Yasmin, pay attention.'

You need to know about Yasmin. She lives opposite my house, on the other side of the railway line. I used to speak to her in primary school all the time, she used to be top of the class. When we started secondary school she started to pretend she wasn't smart. We're in different circles now.

Yasmin smirked and elbowed her boyfriend, Dean, as Mr Roth looked away.

Dean's got tattoos of black fire inked up his arms, and a broken nose from a fight he had last year in the canteen. In year eleven he was at the bottom of all his classes because he enjoys tormenting others more than learning. The only reason he's even in Sixth form is because the school is paid per student.

'Your task,' Mr Roth continued, 'is to create a report of why the Victorians thought this was the ideal place to build a factory. This essay will form part of your coursework so don't waste your time. Keep in mind our distance from the city and the, ah… natural resources,' he glanced at the river. 'You have half an hour before we need to head back.'

I'd actually googled the factory last night so I knew what I was going to say in my essay. No one in the class grouped up with me so I wandered around the site for twenty minutes trying to look busy.

I looked at the luxury flats opposite, trying to think what I would write in my essay. The balcony handrails literally glistened and I could see through the sliding doors into these posh apartments. I swear, there was a bloody yacht being unmoored right outside the apartment.

There was a rustle from the bushes and Dean scrabbled out, twigs tangled in his hair. He blanked me and marched back towards the class, scowling.

I glanced down the riverbank and spotted Yasmin. She was walking towards the water, stumbling on the uneven ground. As she adjusted her hoodie I noticed she was shaking.

'Yasmin?'

Either Yasmin didn't hear me or chose not to answer me. She crossed her arms over her chest and lowered her head facing the river.

I couldn't leave her there, could I?

I clambered through the bushes and landed in the riverbank, caking my shoes in mud.

I could see the water was lapping at Yasmin's trainers. She seemed to be standing with a hunch in her back. She was surrounded by broken bottles, branches and other debris. A different girl to the one I once knew...

'Yasmin?'

'P-piss off.' She picked up a box between her feet and flung it into the river.

I am terrible at comforting people. 'Mr Roth is calling everyone back,' I said, 'we're going home.'

'I'll... be there in a minute.'

Yasmin didn't move. The box drifted back to her feet. As I approached she snatched it up.

'Yasmin? You alright?'

She turned to face me. Tears had ruined her mascara and her bottom lip was quivering. My first thought was that she'd had a fight with Dean. Then I saw the box in her hand.

A pregnancy test.

Henry (Admin1)

Thursday 25 January, 13:54.

Norcrest Academy

I'm sorry for ending the last post like that. I was too tired to finish writing it and I'd reached the important part. Yasmin begged me not to tell anyone. Dean watched us return to the class together but didn't any anything. On the way back to school she kept her hood raised, to avoid eye contact with everyone.

When I got home, Mum told me off for "ruining" my trainers. I played with my Scottish Terrier, Wilfred, until Dad came home late from work. After dinner, Mum and Dad wanted to watch the final of a TV series they'd been following so I went to my room and wrote up the last post.

This is my normal school day. I wake up to the sound of the four minutes past seven train to Cannon Street rushing by my window. Wilfred jumps all over me and tugs at the covers until I'm out of bed. Mum will be watching TV and complaining about the news. Dad will be getting ready for work. After I've drained a gallon of tea and gotten dressed into my suit I take the bus to Sixth form.

My tutor is Mr Sandil. He's nice but he's too busy shouting at the class to be quiet and working his way through the morning announcements to actually help us with anything. The announcements normally consist of how our sports teams are doing, a latest topic in the news like a war or a memorial of some sort and then a pop quiz because how else would you want to start your day?

Joe and Adam have been in my tutor group since year seven. Joe is a coder. He keeps saying that when he leaves school he's going to create codes for computer games as a job. His hair curls back in ringlets at his neck, he gets a lot of shit for it and I don't know why he doesn't get it cut.

Adam is one of the smartest boys in Sixth form. He's also a prefect which means that twice a term he has to attend a meeting with the other prefects, senior teachers and heads of departments and explain what we, the students, think is wrong with the school and what can be done to fix it. Nothing we suggest is ever done and the teachers give us things no one asked for like extra textbooks in the library or benches on the school field.

On Thursdays, I start my day with double history, my least favourite subject. My teacher is Mrs Barton who is also head of Sixth form. She is empty of all emotion apart from wrath and fury. We're studying the history of Germany before World War One. We literally read from the text book and then practice writing essay answers. Adam is in this class so on the rare occasions we do group work I always try to partner up with him. I think everyone hates the class equally but we try not to show it. We don't like Mrs Barton for a variety of reasons, my reason is that the first time she taught us she said that teaching "hormonal teenagers" was a challenge of "herculean proportions" but she would try her best to educate us.

At twenty past eleven, after Mrs Barton has cut into our break by ticking off our completed homework on her infamous spreadsheet, I go to the IT room. What I need to explain about my school is that it's massive. It was called Norcrest School until last year, now it's called The Norcrest Academy. They had to change to an academy to receive more funding from the government but nothing changed for us. Every five years they would open a new building meaning that around a quarter of the school isn't in use.

There's a corridor under the maths department that hosts several disused IT classrooms. Few people come down this end of the school so most break and lunch times Adam, Joe and I go into one of these classrooms and log in to the computers. Some of the computers are old and I mean thick screen old. There's rubbish behind the monitors, sweet wrappers and empty bottles but it's worth it because we're rarely disturbed.

I logged on to Facebook and browsed Yasmin's wall. She hadn't posted anything since last night but the messenger system showed she had been online an hour ago.

Our next lesson was double English. The theme of our exam question this year is "love throughout the ages" which means we have to read books set in different time periods about different kinds of love. Romantic, unrequited, family, friendship, those sort of things. At the moment Mrs Hughes, our English teacher, wants us to read *Frankenstein* and study the love between father and son.

Then we had our lunch break. Joe, Adam and I went to the chip shop.

'I've already aced my English exam,' Joe claimed as we passed through the school reception.

'What, you read *Frankenstein*?' I asked.

'Nah mate, I know all about love.'

'Unrequited,' Adam coughed. 'Seriously though have you two read it?'

'Nah,' Joe said. 'Is there a film I can watch?'

On the way back from the chip shop we walked past a car parked by the school gate. Yasmin's friends Chelsea and Megan were sitting on the back seat shrouded by cigarette smoke. Dean sat in the front passenger seat and a boy who looked like Hagrid on drugs sat behind the steering wheel. I tried to see if Yasmin was inside.

Dean spotted me and flicked me the finger. Chelsea and Megan howled with laughter.

'Fuckin' stinks,' Joe muttered. 'I'm surprised they don't choke.'

Henry (Admin1)

Thursday, 25 January, 18:54.

Norcrest Academy continued

I had enough time to publish the last post before going to my final lesson of the day, general studies. It isn't too bad, we're taught how to think differently and construct an argument. The problem is, our teacher said that this only works in general studies land and never in the real world. I don't know anyone in the class so I watched them debate why some people believe in conspiracy theories and others don't until the bell rang.

I was fighting my way through the bottleneck at the school gates when hand clamped onto my shoulder.

'Did you tell them?' Yasmin demanded.

'Who?'

'Adam and fucking Joe.'

'No, I've not told anyone.' She was so close I could smell her perfume.

'Not even your parents, yeah?' She snatched my hand and pulled me through the school gates. I was suddenly aware of how sweaty I was and I wished I'd sprayed deodorant before leaving class.

'No. Who else knows about it?'

Yasmin dragged me to the other side of the road. The bus braked and the driver blasted his horn at us but Yasmin didn't seem to notice. 'Just me,' she said.

'Shit, whose is it?' I couldn't resist glancing at her stomach. If there was a bump, her hoodie masked it.

'You can't tell anyone about this, yeah? Because... oh Jesus-'

'We should move, people are looking,' I said.

The bus rolled past, students from the younger years had their noses pressed against the windows, jeering anybody in sight. I didn't mind being seen with Yasmin but Joe and Adam would be bound to ask me about it if they found out. Yasmin lead me down a side street.

'How long have you been pregnant for?' I asked her.

'A couple of months, I think.'

'Jesus Christ.' I wanted to ask if it was Dean's. Instead I said, 'What are you gonna do?'

'I don't fucking know. I'm too young to be pregnant.' Yasmin collapsed onto me and sobbed into my shoulder. I held her, almost hugging her and let her cry, because I didn't know what else to do. I wanted to tell Yasmin that getting pregnant was a stupid thing to do but it didn't think it would be helpful. We'd had two other girls in our school become pregnant and they both moved away afterwards. I can't remember how long we stood there, Yasmin shaking in my arms. Eventually she spoke.

'You need to come over mine, after school tomorrow, yeah? We can talk about it then.'

'Yeah, okay.'

I don't know why Yasmin told me this. I like to think she knows she can trust me but I've hardly spoken to her for the past five years or so. I promised her I wouldn't tell my parents until after we met up on Friday.

Thursday, 25 January, 20:26.

Driving lessons

If I'd wanted to tell Mum about it when I got home, I didn't get a chance. When I shut the front door, she started going on about driving lessons.

'Even if you stop them nearer your exams you can start them again afterwards,' she kept saying. Her and Dad have wanted me to start driving lessons for ages. It's fine I guess, everyone else in Sixth form is doing them. You see lots of driving instructor cars parked around the school. We wasted an hour googling driving schools before said I would just ask Joe who his instructor was.

Henry (Admin1)

Friday, 26 January, 16:21.

Geography class

Grace Upshaw is in my tutor group and I sit next to her in geography. Mr Sandil told me to buddy up with her when she joined the school in year nine. Grace made friends with girls in the higher years but since they left she's drifted back to my social circle.

'What do you think of this Mills essay then?' Grace asked me as Mr Sandil started the morning announcements. 'I wasn't even there. I don't know what to write.' I was about to explain it but Grace cut me off, 'I've only written about what I've seen online, my essay is only seven pages. How long's yours?'

'Four.'

Luckily Mr Sandil asked Grace about her holiday. Grace's dad had a business trip in Shanghai and had taken his family, as Grace started talking about her trip I slipped into the seat beside Joe.

'Who's your driving instructor?' I asked. 'Mum's going on about me booking lessons.'

Joe gave me a business card from his pocket.

Colin Grim - Driving instructor.

'He's really good,' Joe said, 'He lets you go fast on the dual carriageways when you get to that bit. He told me I'm basically ready to do my exam now. I just need to book a date for it.'

I can see Joe becoming a boy racer when he gets his own car.

I phoned Colin during my lunch break and we agreed he'll give me a two hour lesson after school Monday night.

Henry (Admin1)

Friday, 26 January, 22:39.
Yasmin's house

I'd told Mum I was going to a revision class. When the school bell sounded at the end of the day I took my normal bus home but got off one stop earlier. I walked across the railway footbridge and knocked at Yasmin's house.

She opened the front door a crack.

'Hey, you okay?' I asked.

Yasmin was wearing her hoodie again but she looked more composed than yesterday. 'Fine,' Yasmin said opening the door. You want anything to drink?'

'Nah, I'm good.'

I'd only been in Yasmin's house once before, for a primary school birthday party. The house was smaller than I remembered but her front room was bigger than mine and hosted a flat screen TV in the corner. A settee faced the window, in front of that was a stained coffee table. The wallpaper was the same dull yellow that I remembered but now it had become sun bleached and the pictures on the mantelpiece of Yasmin as a child had been updated. Around the mantelpiece, next to the TV, were framed certificates of contract completions but I didn't understand the wording.

'What are these?' I asked when Yasmin returned from the kitchen with a can of coke. A cigarette dangled between the thumb and forefinger.

'Oh, Dad's an interior designer. He likes to put his completed contracts on the walls.'

Yasmin crossed the room, opened the front room window and started to smoke.

'Cool. My Dad's a builder,' I said, 'he works around the city mostly.'

Yasmin grunted.

I watched the way the smoke drifted through her lips. 'Should you be smoking while you're… you know?'

'Fuck off. Just fuck off.' She threw the cig out the window, 'I'm… trying to cut down,' she admitted.

'Have you had a scan or anything?

'Nah, not yet. I've been around the local clinics and hospitals and stuff. Picked these up,' she pointed to a pile of leaflets on the coffee table. I examined one, the front cover showed of a silhouette of a pregnant woman within which was written the title: Pregnancy Advice.

'Ok. I've done some googling,' I said before realising how crap that sounded.

'Oh good, go on, then. What do you think I should do?'

'Right… so basically you've got three options. You could have the baby.'

'No, I'm eighteen, for Christ's sake. I don't wanna to look like one of those girls you see on *Teen Mum*.'

Yasmin looked nothing like those girls. I'd actually Googled some baby names as well, I liked the names Charis for a girl and Liam for a boy. Maybe I'd use those names in the future? I wasn't going to say anything though because it would sound really creepy. 'What about adoption? When it's born, you could give it away?'

'I don't want to be carrying it around inside me like a parasite for nine months.'

I thought that was a very harsh way to describe it. 'What do you know about the baby?' I asked.

'It's not a baby. It's a thing and I don't want it. I don't know nothin' and I don't wanna know. Like I said, I've not had any tests or anythin' like that.'

I didn't like the way she was dehumanising it but Yasmin looked terrified so I didn't say anything. I glanced at her stomach again as though the bump would have become visible since Wednesday.

'Do you know who the father is?' I asked. I wanted to leave, I wanted to be anywhere else but here but I couldn't just walk out. I could feel vomit, caused by my own fear, rising in my throat but forced myself to keep it down. Christ knows how Yasmin felt.

'Dean, obviously. Who else would it be?'

'Does he know?' I asked.

'No. He'd go mental, wouldn't he?'

I hate Dean but Jesus…

'What about your dad?'

'Dad's visiting my sister at Uni.'

'Okay, okay. How long have you known?'

'Since the school trip.'

'Oh fuck…'

Yasmin lit another cigarette. 'I took the test on the riverbank in the bushes.'

'Dean was with you?'

'He didn't know what I was doing. He thought I needed a piss. I couldn't stand not knowing, y'know? I wanted to be certain.'

'Couldn't you wait until you got home?'

'No, listen to me. I had to do it there. I had to know. I had to.'

I thought she was about to cry. Instead Yasmin took another drag of her cig. I examined the crumpled leaflets.

'Do you want... an abortion?' I asked. The word had been highlighted inside the leaflet.

'Maybe. I dunno.'

'Fuck. Couldn't you ask like, a teacher or a doctor or something? Your dad-'

'My dad would kill me. I'm gonna to tell someone, yeah, but not yet. For now we keep this between us, alright?'

I didn't want to keep it between us. I wanted nothing more than to ask an adult... or anyone really, what to do. I remembered that last year two girls in year thirteen became pregnant and they both had to move out of the area. I don't want that to happen to Yasmin But if I did tell someone, how much of an arsehole to Yasmin would I be?

'Okay,' I said.

Henry (Admin1)

Monday, 29 January, 13:29.

Mrs Saunders

I still haven't told anyone about Yasmin's baby. Mr Sandil asked if I was alright in tutor time because I looked distant.

'Fine,' I said, 'headache.'

Mr Sandil nodded and continued the announcements, 'Tickets for the end of year prom are now on sale.' He looked around the classroom as though expecting us to leap to our feet. 'They are twenty pounds a ticket and it's in the Vaughan Hotel. Mrs Barton has told me that your behaviour and attendance rate will affect your chances of being allowed entrance on the night.'

'I need to go to prom,' Adam whispered.

'Why? Because you're a prefect?'

'Yeah.'

Adam loves being a prefect. He posts any announcements Mrs Barton has for the year group on Facebook and literally the day he was made a prefect he added it to his CV. I'm not really fussed, if I'm honest. It sounds like extra work but Adam enjoys it. Joe thinks it's just a joke.

'I ain't going,' Joe said, 'I don't want to see anyone here again. Why would I want to go to a party with them? It's gonna to be shit anyway.'

'There'll be free drinks?' I added but Joe shrugged.

'I've got drinks at home. I could throw a brilliant party if I wanted to. Just the three of us,'

'Pass.'

'Oh, and what'd you know about parties?' Joe sneered.

'I went to Glastonbury last year with my family.'

'Yeah, well you didn't really experience it if you didn't camp there, did you?' Joe said.

Adam rolled his eyes and I stopped listening to them.

I haven't told you about Mrs Saunders. She's the school counselor, she's the teacher who put me in contact with Doctor West. She caught me going to my English class this morning and brought me into her office.

'You okay, Henry?' she asked as she closed her office door. Mrs Saunder's office is more like a cupboard. Her desk takes up most of the room, there's only space for two chairs, one for each of us. The walls are covered with cheesy inspirational posters of sunsets and palm trees and that kind of crap. I could hear the rabble of students on the other side of the door walking past to their lessons.

'I'm fine,' I said.

'How are things?

'Everything's going okay, thanks.' I've been thinking about what happens after Sixth form. It's an empty void in my future. I don't think anyone in the year group is prepared for what comes next.

'Are your lessons going well?

'I'm doing okay in everything apart from history but I've never been good at that.'

'Last year you said history was your favourite subject.'

That's another nice thing about Mrs Saunders, she remembers what you say. 'Yeah but this year we're doing boring parts of history. The parts nobody cares about.'

'I think you'll find people disagree with you there Henry but we'll save that conversation for our next meeting?'

She pencilled me in for a meeting with her tomorrow during one of my free periods and then gave me a note to say why I was late to lesson.

Henry (Admin1)

Monday, 29 January, 22:09.

First driving lesson

Colin the driving instructor arrived as soon as I had finished getting changed after school. Mum and I met him at the front door.

Colin's car had his name and phone number printed across it along with L plates on the bonnet and boot. I couldn't help but notice the various bumps and dents along the bodywork of his car.

'He's nervous, bless,' I heard Mum whisper to Colin at the front door.

Colin just laughed. 'Have you ever driven before?' he asked me.

'My Dad let me reserve his car in a car park once,' I said.

'He should be on his way home,' Mum said, 'your dad, I mean. Must be stuck in traffic.'

'Not to worry,' Colin said, 'We'll stick to the back streets.'

Colin drove me to Hillberry Road where there was little traffic. I kept my feet as close to my seat as I could, I was scared of accidentally touching the dual controls. When we pulled over Colin could see I was nervous but he was cool about it. We spoke about controls, road safety, checking mirrors and then we swapped seats and Colin told me to start the engine.

'Clutch down, twist the key.'

The car's engine roared into life.

'Clutch down, first gear and release the handbrake.'

The car rolled forwards. It felt like I was in a Formula One racing car even though I knew I was going at 4 mph.

Colin drove me home and asked when I wanted my next lesson to be. I booked it for next week Tuesday. Mum had finished cooking dinner and Dad explained he had only gotten home two minutes ago.

'We might have just passed each other on the road,' he said. Then he asked me what sort of car Colin had and where I drove. When we finished eating he showed me where to put my hands on the steering wheel by using a dinner plate.

Henry (Admin1)

Wednesday 31 January, 13:59.

Essay feedback

Not much to report today.

I've not heard back from Yasmin. I've not seen her since Friday and she's not answered any of my Facebook messages.

Joe asked me how my driving lesson went in tutor time.

'It was good, yeah,' I said. 'We drove up and down Hillberry Road.'

'He took me to the same place when I started lessons,' Joe said,' all the driving instructors go there.'

I could imagine someone living on Hillberry Road looking out their window and seeing three or four learner cars prowling around the streets.

I've had three essays back today. Mrs Hughes gave me back my analysis on *Frankenstein*. She said that she likes my deep reading of the source material but the way I write is the way I speak. She wants us to study Shakespeare's Sonnets 18 and 130 for our next lesson.

Mrs Barton gave me back my history essay and said that I had misunderstood the question. The question was something like, What was the stability of Germany like in the 1900? I argued that it was stable because that's how I read the question but apparently it wasn't. She wants to me rewrite my answer for the next lesson because at the moment it's ungradable. Mrs Barton also set a second essay from today's lesson. Name the contributing factors that lead to the Fall of Prussia. I'm not really worried about general studies but geography is trickier. The geography coursework is in four parts, but we only have the final part left to submit. It's due in three weeks. I need to proofread twenty pages and write an essay about aquaculture in 20th century England. Mr Roth gave my essay on Milton's Mill a C. Grace was given an A because she went into more detail about the history of the Mill.

Henry (Admin1)

Friday, 2 February, 19:30.

Mock results

I picked up my mock results in the Common Room after school. I should explain about our Common Room. We have five leather settees that have most of the leather picked off, a faulty radio, and a dozen computers. Mrs Barton's office is at the end of the Common Room. The noise of the rest of the year group is always distracting which is why I prefer to work in the IT room.

We filed into the Common Room and queued up for Mrs Barton to give us our results. We did the mock exams before Christmas. I knew I had terrible results before I had even finished my exams.

History: D

English Literature: D

General studies: C

Geography: C

Mrs Saunders said that I shouldn't compare my grades to anyone else's like Adam because he always get straight A's. I still think I've got terrible results, all the time I spent revising over Christmas was wasted. Even Joe got a C in English. Because I don't know what I want to do after Sixth form yet, Mrs Saunders and I agreed that I should aim for straight C's. Then I'll have plenty of options when I want to make a decision.

Here is the percentage for exams and coursework in each of my subjects:

History. Exam 100%. Coursework 0%

English Literature. Exam 100%. Coursework 0%

General studies. Exam 70% Coursework 30%

Geography. Exam 50% Coursework 50%

I know I can get C's on all of my coursework but my exam grades will drag me down. I know what to write in my essays and I know what points I want to say but I can't put my thoughts into words. I hate exams but that's where you get most of your marks.

Henry (Admin1)

Tuesday, 8 February, 16:23.

Dad left

I was in my room rewriting my Germany essay for Mrs. Barton and waiting for Colin to arrive when I heard raised voices from downstairs. I thought it was the TV but then I heard the front door slam and a few minutes later Mum came into my room.

'Hen, sweetheart. I've got some bad news.' She was shaking and her eyes were red but I was too shocked to get out of my chair. Wilfred was running around her feet, yapping.

Mum picked Wilfred up, gave him a cuddle and then buried her head in his hair and burst into tears.

I don't remember much after that but I got the story out of Mum between sobs. Dad had been having an affair with his manager at work. Her name is Linda. Mum didn't know what Linda looked like but Dad had said they had been exchanging Facebook messages, texts and had been sleeping together for months. That's why Dad had been late home most nights.

I have a large family but Mum is closest to her brother, Patrick, who lives twenty minutes away. When Mum called him she couldn't explain what had happened because she couldn't stop crying but Uncle Patrick must of realised it was something serious because he come over straight away. He arrived at the same time Colin pulled up and thought Colin was something to do with Dad. He started having a massive go at Colin until Mum brought Uncle Patrick inside, apologised to Colin and closed the door. I watched as Colin drove away, bewildered and then I tried to explain to Uncle Patrick what had happened.

When I came downstairs the next morning Mum said, 'We think it's a good idea if you didn't go to school today, Hen.' She looked a little better than yesterday, she had makeup on but a forced smile. Uncle Patrick was cooking breakfast, he's a chef in a Harvester.

I hadn't even thought about school. I'd been up all night playing Skyrim. 'Ok.'

'We could go round the park instead,' she suggested.

'That's fine. Should I phone Doctor West and tell him what's happened?'

'Shit, yeah. I forgot. Tell Doctor West, see what he says and if he says it's okay we can go to the park after breakfast.'

I haven't explained who Doctor West is yet. I promise I will.

Uncle Patrick has a bad knee and had to stop at every bench because he left his cane at his house. He and Mum chatted with all the dog walkers so we were in the park for two hours. We didn't actually do a lot apart from walk and talk but that was alright. Mum kept smiling but you could tell she didn't mean it. We were about to go home when Dad rang my mobile. I was standing at the edge of the empty playground and Uncle Patrick and Mum were making a fuss over a passing Dalmatian.

'Hello?'

'Henry.' His voice sounded guff, like he'd just woken up. 'Hey, are you okay?'

'Yeah. I'm fine.'

'And your mum?'

'She's with Uncle Patrick. He's staying with us for a couple of days.'

'Ah, alright then. That's good. He'll keep her on her feet for a while, won't he? Listen. I'm going to stay out of the way for a week or two. I'll ring you soon, yeah?'

'Sure.'

'You gonna be alright?'

'I'm fine, it's mum I'm worried about.'

'She has Uncle Patrick to look after her, don't she? Don't worry. I'll see you soon and I'll tell you all about it then, okay?'

'Ok, love you.'

'You too.'

Henry (Admin1)

Wednesday, 9 February, 13:19.

Meeting with Mrs Saunders

When I came into tutor Mr Sandil was talking about a Thorpe Park trip at the end of the year. I don't like roller coasters anyway so I wasn't really listening. I sat down between Joe and Adam, I'd texted them yesterday and told them what had happened.

'You alright, mate?' Adam whispered as Mr Sandil started talking about how many students could go on the trip.

'What happened?' Joe asked.

'Dad's been having an affair with a manager at his work.'

'Shit,' Joe breathed, 'how long?'

'I dunno. He didn't say.'

I was halfway through explaining what had happened when Mrs Saunders came in and asked to see me.

'I heard about your dad,' she said as we walked down the corridor towards her office. 'You should have come and seen me when you came in this morning.'

When we reached her office, I told Mrs Saunders all about Dad leaving. It was hard to tell how much Doctor West had said to her already.

When I finished she asked, 'what about the rest of your family? How's everyone else taking it?'

'Mum said this morning that she is going to have a James Bond marathon with my Uncle.'

'Your Uncle's staying with you?'

'Yeah he's there to look after Mum. Wilfred is pretty sad too. You know, Wilfred?'

'Your dog?'

'Yeah. He keeps whining at the door for Dad to come back...' I didn't realise I had been crying. Mrs Saunders handed me a box of tissues.

'Have you heard from your dad since he left, Henry?' she asked.

'Yeah. He called to make sure I was okay when we were up the park yesterday.'

'That shows he still cares about you, doesn't it?'

She then told me that divorce and breakups are a normal part of adult life. Most marriages end in divorce apparently. When the bell rang she asked if there was anything else I wanted to tell her and then let me go to class. She made me promise that if I ever feel like I needed to talk I would come to her office.

When the bell went at the end of our history lesson Mrs Barton asked me to carry the spare textbooks back to her office with her.

'Are you alright?' she asked as we forged a path through the corridor, 'I heard your dad left.'

No tact, straight to the point.

'Yeah, I'm fine.' Some people, when their parents leave or someone in their family dies, shut down. At least I was still operating.

'Are you sure? Because if it isn't, if you need help, you can drop into my office anytime.'

'Thanks.'

'You won't have to worry about the essay on the stability of Germany,' Mrs Barton said, 'but you'll still need to finish the Prussia essay.' She then told me what pages I needed to read in order to catch up with the rest of the class.

Henry (Admin1)

Thursday, 10 February, 15:15.

Money problems

Uncle Patrick sleeps on the settee. It's nice having him around but it makes things feel more different than they already are. Me, Mum and Dad had a routine but now we've had to work around Uncle Patrick. He also watches the football on maximum volume and he's really nosy. I was playing Skyrim in my bedroom when he came in and said to me.

'What's that you're playing?'

'Skyrim.'

'Ah right, what's it about?'

He didn't understand the story or anything but he kept asking questions so that in the end I had to stop playing and talk to him. He's nice though because he looks after Mum. When she hits a low point, as he calls it, he cheers her up or cooks her something.

When he was out of the house on a shopping trip for us, Mum said to me,

'Henry, now Dad has left we need to bit a careful with our money okay? We don't have a dual income, we don't have his money coming in.'

'Ok.'

'You can't spend it on Itunes every day. You need to be careful.'

'Ok, Mum,'

'No sneaky visits to the chippy or the corner shop or anything like that. No add ons for your games. We can survive, but things are going to be tight for a while, do you understand?'

'Yeah, I understand.'

'Good. Another thing, don't tell Uncle Patrick, ok?'

'I won't.'

I've texted Colin and apologised for Uncle Patrick shouting at him. Colin phoned me back and I explained that we were having a family emergency. He said that was fine and we've booked another lesson next week.

Henry (Admin1)

Saturday, 10 February, 17:01.

Simon

I've seen Yasmin twice this weekend. The first time I was in bed. I had just turned my light out when my phoned vibrated.

Yasmin: You ok?

Wilfred looked up from his bed as I typed back.

Me: I'm okay. Dad left.

The answer came almost at once.

Yasmin: I heard about it at school. Window?

After listening for a moment to see if Mum or Patrick were still awake I snuck out of bed.

Yasmin was wearing pink pajamas. She smiled and waved.

Yasmin: You want to come over 2morrow?

I gave her a thumbs up.

Mum and Uncle Patrick went to the solicitors this morning to ask for legal advice about the divorce. After they left I crossed the footbridge and went to Yasmin's house.

I had to knock five times before Yasmin opened the door.

'Hey,' she was still wearing her pajamas from last night, 'can you go in the front room for a minute?' She let me in and rushed back upstairs.

I didn't know what to do with myself. The leaflets for the clinics weren't there and I couldn't stop thinking about the fact Yasmin wanted an abortion.

I looked at the contract certificates again and noticed a picture I hadn't seen the first time. Yasmin stood grinning on one side of a girl half a head taller dressed in a graduation cap and gown. Next to the girls was Yasmin's dad, he was just as skinny as I remembered but he had now grown a goatee.

I couldn't remember his name at first, the last time I had spoken to him was at Yasmin's birthday party in primary school. Then I heard footsteps on the stairs and saw the same man looking down at me.

'Henry,' Yasmin's dad swooped down the stairs and gave me a man hug as though we were old friends. 'How are you?' He looked around the front room and then peered into the kitchen to see if he had anymore unexpected guests.

'I'm fine, thanks.'

'I'm so sorry, I thought you were Chelsea or Dean or one of her other friends. Do you want a drink?' Before I could answer he bellowed up the stairs, 'Yasmin, Henry's waiting for you!'

I spotted Yasmin's dad's name on one of the certificates, Simon Rivers, and I spoke to him about my A Levels. He didn't know Dad had left because he didn't mention it or maybe he was just being polite. He kept saying that Yasmin hadn't done any revision for her exams and I lied and said I was here to study with her.

'Sorry,' Yasmin muttered when she returned. She'd thrown her hoodie back on.

'You shouldn't have kept Henry waiting, Yasmin. I'm going to be in the study if you need me.'

'Sorry, you alright? What happened with your Dad?' Yasmin asked as Simon trudged upstairs.

I told her about Dad having an affair with his manager and about Uncle Patrick living with us.

'That fucking sucks. I remember when my Mum died. Dad didn't smile for weeks. He's not completely over it actually.'

'How old were you when she died?'

'Just a kid.' Yasmin paused before saying, 'We can talk about it, y'know? Dad can't hear us when he's in his study.' I thought she was talking about my dad but instead Yasmin took out her phone and showed me a website page on teenage pregnancy.

'There's whole groups lobbying for and against abortions.' I said.

'Yeah, I saw them up in London once. They closed a whole road,' Yasmin said. 'But that was years ago, y'know, and I wasn't paying attention.'

She scrolled down the webpage and we saw a protester holding a placard that read Stop killing the innocent. I read some of the other placards the protesters were displaying, some were written in mock blood and one even had a gun pointing at a fetus. There was some seriously dark stuff.

'Is it... murder?' I asked.

'Dunno. Don't think so. I mean, it's not human yet, is it? It's not alive.'

'How far pregnant you are?'

'Second trimester.'

'You need to tell someone,' I said.

'No. Fuck no. We're going to think about it first.'

I googled pregnancy information with Yasmin. The internet said it was legal to have an abortion anytime in the first twenty four weeks in England which meant Yasmin still had time. She kept going on sex ed websites to learn more about the operation but it was the same websites I'd already visited at school.

I lost track of time and when Simon came downstairs and asked Yasmin to nip to the shops to buy something for dinner I realised it had been two hours. I thought it was best that

I left too before Mum and Uncle Patrick returned. Yasmin and I walked to the footbridge together.

'I'll see you in geography on Tuesday, yeah?' I asked.

'Yeah,' Yasmin said. 'Probably.'

I had just gotten home when Mum and Uncle Patrick returned. Mum looked exhausted and Uncle Patrick was furious over something the solicitor had said. We watched the football until they fell asleep, then I wrote this post.

Henry (Admin1)

Monday, 12 February, 16:22.

More homework

Mrs Barton was in a particularly bad mood for my double history lesson this morning and we wrote our essays in silence. She marked our Prussia essays and gave them back to us, I got a D, and then set us more homework to do. We had to read the chapter in our textbooks on Mussolini's rise to power.

I gave in my essays on Shakespeare's sonnets 18 and 130. I probably sound awful for saying this but I can't think of a single situation where poetry is useful apart from Christmas cards and Valentine's day. I'm sure there are people who love poetry and that's fine. I'm not one of them. Mrs Hughes told us to read *The Great Gatsby* for next lesson. She said it was a small book and would only take a few hours to read.

Henry (Admin1)

Tuesday, 13 February, 10:27.

Personal statements

We've been told over the past couple of weeks, to write our personal statements for university or college. No one in my year has finished their statements yet, so Mrs Barton had threatened to cancel our free periods until we'd handed them in.

'I mean, it's not like they actually read them anyway, do they? All they care about is your grades,' Joe said in the Common Room. 'In fact, they don't even care about that. They let you in with shit grades sometimes. Through clearing.'

'Yeah, but a statement can't hurt,' I said. We'd been told to write about the subject we were most passionate about. My favourite subject is geography but I didn't know if I wanted to commit to that after Sixth form.

'You started that book yet, *The Great Gatsby*?' Adam asked.

'Nah, not yet.' I'd meant to read it last night but instead I researched prolife protesters in America. I'd been reading about a case where some hard core protested beat up a woman who'd just left the clinic after her abortion and nearly killed her.

Our conversation subsided as Mrs Barton strode past.

'What have you been doing?' Adam hissed. 'It's due tomorrow.'

'I know what he's been doing,' Joe whispered with a wink. 'Word is, you were at Yasmin's house at the weekend.'

'Who told you that?' I asked.

'Jake saw you two together on Sunday,' Adam said. 'You know, Megan's boyfriend?'

I assumed Jake was the driver of the car I had seen Yasmin and her friends in.

'Does Jake even go to this school?' I asked.

'Nah, he goes to some art college somewhere,' Joe said 'so... what'd you do to her?'

'Fuck off.'

'Did you...? Joe made a circle with one hand and pumped his other hand through the hole.

'Joe!' Mrs Barton snapped and Joe's hands returned to his keyboard.

I knew rumors were going around about me and Yasmin but I'd done my best to ignore them.

That afternoon in geography, Mr Roth set us an essay on volcanic rock that forms part of our coursework, and returned our essays on aquaculture in 20th century England. I got a C. Mr Roth's classroom overlooks the school gates, we could see everyone leaving as we stayed for our revision class.

'Henry,' Grace whispered to me. 'Is it true?'

'What?'

'Is it true you're going out with Yasmin Rivers?'

'No.'

'Everyone's saying you are.'

'Well, I'm not.'

Yasmin wasn't in geography. I could see Jake's car by the school gates but I couldn't see if she was inside.

Henry (Admin1)

Wednesday, 14 February, 23:11.

Patrick has gone home

Uncle Patrick left today. Honestly, I'm glad he's gone. It was nice having him here but he was getting in the way.

'You ring me, if he comes calling, yeah?' he said to Mum as he left. Mum promised that she would but I know she won't. Dad hasn't called us to say when he's coming to pick up his stuff or rung me back. Uncle Patrick said we should bin his stuff but Mum said no.

After Uncle Patrick left, me and Mum watched a film on *Channel Four* and then went to bed. I'm not sure what Mum is going to do tomorrow but we promised that we'll go for a meal in the Harvester, where Uncle Patrick works, after school.

Henry (Admin1)

Thursday, 15 February, 20:28.

Geography Coursework with Yasmin

Yasmin texted me this morning saying she was freaking out about the geography coursework and asked if I could go over and help her with it after school. My final lesson of the day was geography, Yasmin should have been in class but she said she didn't want to see Mr Roth until she had caught up on the coursework and would meet me at the school gates. We agreed to meet at the school gates at three. I'd been talking to Grace throughout geography and she followed me to the gates.

'I'm thinking of doing an art course when I leave,' Grace was saying, 'or maybe advanced maths at uni. I can't decide. I don't want to go to uni too far away.'

I could see Yasmin sitting in Jake's car and she looked pissed that Grace was with me.

'Have you got any plans for after school, Hen?' Grace asked.

'I'm busy tonight.'

'No, I meant after Sixth form.'

'Oh, no. Not yet.'

'My brother went to uni but he dropped out in the first year.'

'Right.'

'He said it was really hard living away from home. He said he felt he was going to go insane.'

'Right.'

'I might stay on an extra year if I can. Year fourteen.'

'Cool, yeah.'

After a few minutes, when the jeers and shouts of Jake, Chelsea and Megan were too much to ignore, I saw Yasmin get out of the car and march towards us.

'Hey.' It sounded more like a challenge than a greeting.

'We were just talking about after Sixth form,' Grace said, 'do you know what do you want to do?'

'We were talking about staying on an extra year, into year fourteen if we need to,' I said.

'Ready to go?' Yasmin asked me.

'Oh.. yeah... Grace, I'll catch you later. Okay?'

Grace blinked. 'O... okay.'

'Let's go,' Yasmin muttered. She turned away from Grace and walked towards the bus stop, past Jake's car.

I followed her. 'Why'd you talk to Grace like that?' I asked.

Yasmin shrugged.

'Fuck her hard,' Jake bellowed as we passed.

Megan and Chelsea blew us kisses from the backseat.

Yasmin lowered her head, I felt my cheeks grow warm.

'Piss off.' I couldn't think of anything else to say. I was glad Dean wasn't there. Yasmin tugged on my sleeve to keep me walking.

'Jesus, he's a stress head, ain't he?' I heard Megan say to a chorus of laughter.

'I've told them to stop' Yasmin said as Jake sounded the car horn and pulled off the kerb.

'Have you told anyone about it yet?'

'No'

'Jesus, you need to-'

'Leave it.'

The back windows were open a crack and I could see the cigarette smoke trickling out. Jake swerved out back onto the pavement to avoid an oncoming orange car. The driver shouted but Jake had already raced away.

'Idiot,' Yasmin muttered.

The car slowed as it approached. Mr Roth waved as he drove past.

'Bastards are lucky they didn't crash into him,' Yasmin said as Jake avoided an oncoming bus by mounting the kerb again. I like to think that Chelsea and Megan dropped their cigarettes.

'He's given us our coursework tasks, by the way. Mr Roth I mean.'

'Great.'

'No, they're really simple. It's a couple of reports and stuff and only one big essay.'

'How long till it's due in?' Yasmin asked as the bus pulled up before us.

'End of the month.'

Simon was home when we arrived but retreated upstairs when we said we wanted to do our coursework. I explained to Yasmin that most people who gave the coursework in got A Stars because it was really simple, just time consuming.

Yasmin said doing it would take one thing off her mind and talked about how stressed she was. We started work at four and didn't finish till six when the pizza we ordered arrived.

When I got home, Mum was waiting.

'Where the hell have you been?'

'With Yasmin doing coursework?' I said. Then I remembered I was meant to be having a meal with Mum tonight. 'Shit, I didn't-'

'I've been ringing you.'

I fished my phone out of my pocket. Twelve missed calls.

Mum shouted for a bit and when I'd told her I had already eaten at Yasmins' she went to bed crying.

Henry (Admin1)

Friday, 16 February, 11:22.
Dad wants to meet up

Dad just called. He seemed to know that Uncle Patrick has left so Mum must have told him. Mum spoke to him in her room and told me that they'd arranged a day for him to pick up his stuff from the house but I would be at school.

'I'll stay at home that day,' I said.

Mum went fucking mental and kept saying how important my final year in Sixth form was and that I couldn't afford a single day off. Complete bullshit. One of Joe's friends who did their A Levels last year didn't go to any of the classes because they hated their teacher. They taught themselves at home from the textbook and the teacher taught the class the wrong part of the syllabus. Everyone failed apart from Joe's friend, who got an A star. Anyway, Mum said Dad wanted to meet me outside Primark on Saturday to have something to drink and I told her that was okay but I still wanted to meet him at the house when he picked up his stuff.

Henry (Admin1)

Friday, 16 February, 18:36.

Dad's stuff

Dad's picked up his stuff. I was planning on bunking my lessons if I knew Dad would be at home there but apparently he just turned up. I think Mum organised it yesterday and didn't tell me but I can't prove it. Mum said that she helped him load his stuff into a van and that Dad explained he was living with Linda now. Mum said Dad would tell me about it tomorrow.

I'm still doing my driving lessons. I know I haven't written about them in a while but that's because there hasn't really been a lot to say. I've been practicing going up and down the gears. Today we focused on junctions. I was scared I'd crash into someone but Colin said that because we were in a learner car people would be nicer to us. We made the turn onto the high street, joined the flow of traffic and then took the next turning off.

It was okay, actually.

Henry (Admin1)

Friday, 16 February, 20:11.

Harvester

When we arrived for dinner the Harvester was almost empty. Patrick came out of the kitchen, dressed in his chef's uniform complete with hat and said hello. He was glistening with sweat, I think he said he had been cooking for five hours. He told the waiter who served us to give us extra portions of whatever we asked for.

Because of the vouchers Uncle Patrick gave us we only had to pay for our drinks.

Henry (Admin1)

Saturday, 17 February, 20:09.

Meeting Dad

Mum dropped me off outside Primark and said she would pick me up when I'd texted her. I think she was scared of what Dad would say to me. I waited on a bench outside Primark and after five minutes Dad arrived.

'Alright Henry?'

He looked as if he had gotten fatter in the weeks away from me and Mum or maybe I was imagining it. He hadn't shaved and he was wearing a coat I hadn't seen before, probably something Linda had brought him.

'Hey, Dad.'

He gave me a bear hug and then we sort of looked at each other.

'I think it's about time you had a proper drink, Henry. Fancy coming down the pub for a bit?'

I'd sampled several beers and ales at Joe's Brother's party but Dad didn't know this. The pub was called *The Three Bells* and looked like a tip. Five drunk boys were singing at the bar, another group of men around Dad's age were arguing over a snooker table and the table we choose was covered in crumbs and spilt drink.

'You'll like this,' Dad said plonking a glass of beer before me. The foam dribbled down the side of the glass. I look a sip, it tasted horrible.

Dad took a mouthful of his drink, swallowed, and sighed slouching in his chair.

'Right,' he said, 'I'm staying with Linda now. She has a house a few roads away from the high street. Do you want to see a picture of her?'

He pulled out his phone and loaded a photo. It could have been a Facebook profile picture, Linda looked like she was in her mid thirties or early forties. Brown hair in a bun, a wide smile. She looked pretty I guess.

'What's she like?' I asked.

'She's nice.

'What about your friends? Josh and...'

'Joe and Adam are okay. Adam wants to go to Uni but he doesn't know what he wants to study. Joe wants to get a job in coding and stay out of education.'

'What about you?'

'I dunno yet.'

There was a TV in the corner of the pub and as the match began more people began to drift inside until there was standing room only. The match was Arsenal vs Man United and I watched it in silence expect for when Arsenal scored a goal and I cheered along with everyone else. When the match finished Dad said he had to get back to Linda's and we pushed our way to the exit.

'How's your mum? Your uncle's saying over, isn't he?' Dad asked as I texted Mum to pick me up.

'Yeah, he's gone home now but he's told Mum he can pop over whenever she needs him to.'

'Good, he'll understand it all. He's separated, isn't he?'

'What do you mean understand?'

'Adult relationships. It's... I mean. Sometimes things work out and sometimes they don't. You following?'

I shook my head.

'You know how everyone is searching for the one? Well when your mum is ready she can find her one. The next one. The one to make her happy.'

I was going to ask what he meant but Mum pulled up on the opposite side of the road. Dad have me a hug and left.

'How was he?' she asked as I opened the car door.

'He's fine.'

'Did he ask about us? Did he ask how you were getting on at school?'

'Yeah he wanted to know what me and all my friends were up to. He asked about you too.'

'What did he say?'

'He asked how you were.'

'And did you tell him I was doing alright?'

'Yeah.'

'Good.'

Henry (Admin1)

Monday, 19 February, 11:23.

References

When he had taken the register Mr Sandil reminded us that the prom tickets were still available.

'Mrs Barton has asked me to tell you that she had begun to write your university references.'

Mr Sandil smiled as though this news was a great surprise.

'What's she saying in our references?' Grace asked.

'She'll tell the university if you're a good student or not, what your grades are expected to be.'

When the bell rang for the start of period one, Mr Sandil was still issuing announcements.

'One more thing. If everyone doesn't give in their personal statement by the end of the week then Mrs Barton says she will start emailing your parents about them.'

'We've not had enough time to write them,' Joe whined but Mr Sandil's class was already at his door and ordered us to leave.

I've finished reading The Great Gatsby. Mrs Hughes says that the message of the book depends on how you read it. I think it's a tragic love story, like Romeo and Juliet. I've written my reflective essay on Gatsby and I'll give it to Mrs Hughes in the next lesson.

Henry (Admin1)

Monday, 19 February, 23:14.

Cowards

Yasmin sent me a Facebook message asking to meet up after school to go over baby stuff.

'You okay?' I asked when she opened the door.

'Course.'

'You weren't in class last week.'

'Oh, I couldn't be arsed,' she scoffed. 'Come in, I've got some things to show you.'

Simon came downstairs to say hello, he looked delighted that I'd come over again. Yasmin listened for the sound of his study door closing when he went back upstairs.

'You've not told him?'

'Leave it Henry. Look at this.' Yasmin opened her laptop.

The website had the title The Mistveil Clinic typed at the top of the page. The homepage listed the services the clinic provided on the right hand side while the left showed a picture of the clinic, a converted detached house.

'Look,' Yasmin said again and clicked on a link. The page reloaded to show a scan of a fetus on her laptop. 'They sort of suck it, out,' she said, 'like a hoover on your vagina. You can have local or general anesthetic, if you want. You don't even need an overnight stay in hospital, they send you home the same day.'

I couldn't imagine it. I couldn't imagine Yasmin on an operation table, I couldn't imagine what sort of device would be used to suck the fetus out and didn't like the way Yasmin was describing the living thing inside her as "it".

'Isn't there a simpler way?' I asked 'Can you take a pill or a tablet?'

'I'll have an allergic reaction,' Yasmin said, 'trust me, I will. Anyway it's too late for that.'

I thought that was a really shitty excuse but I didn't say anything. 'What about the after effects?' I asked.

'Some women get depression but that sometimes happens after they've given birth anyway.' Yasmin said. She took the crumpled pregnancy leaflets out of her hoodie pocket handed them to me.

'Where is this clinic?'

'At the end of the L43 bus route. It's, like, twenty minutes. There's a map on the website.'

'Look though, are you sure about this?'

'Yeah.'

'There isn't a reset button. '

'Do you think I don't know that?' Yasmin clammed the laptop shut.

'Do you not want to tell someone?'

'No. No one else needs to know, do they?'

I can't put the fear I felt into words. Yasmin was saying something about how if people knew she was pregnant it would ruin her life and her dad would never forgive her. I nodded but it was as though I was on autopilot.

'I've got it,' Yasmin bellowed up the stairs as the doorbell rang.

While Yasmin was out of the room I debated running upstairs and blurting it all out to Simon. I didn't because as much as I hate it, it is Yasmin's choice.

'Fuck off Dean!'

I sprinted to the doorway in time to see Yasmin slam the door against Dean's foot.

'Let me in.' Dean was wearing a leather jacket and a motorbike helmet with the visor up. Yasmin threw her whole weight against the door as Dean stuck his arm inside the gap and tried to push his way through.

'Who's that?' Dean howled as he spotted me. 'Who's that? Who's that? Who the fuck is that?'

'Piss off, Dean.'

'Henry,' Dean roared. 'You're fucking Henry? Over me? Me?' Dean punched his chest like Tarzan and Yasmin slammed the door.

'Christ, he doesn't think we're fucking, does he?' Yasmin asked.

I failed to say anything. My lips moved but no words came.

Simon bolted down the stairs. 'Who's that?' he demanded as Dean hammered on the door.

I retreated to the safety of the stairs. Neither of them noticed.

'Dean.'

'What's he doing here?'

'I dunno, how should I know?''

'Ok. Wait in the front room.'

I fled to the settee with Yasmin and watched through the front room window as Simon flung open the door. Dean was holding his helmet and had his mouth open, midway through swearing.

'Where's Yasmin?

'She doesn't want to talk to you, Dean. Please, leave.'

'Where is she? And where's Henry?'

'If you don't go away I'll call the police.' There was a pause before Simon added, 'Don't think I won't. I don't think a spot on your criminal record would look good when applying for college, do you?'

I knew that Dean already had a criminal record for stealing and assault and I doubted he would care if another charge was added. To my surprise Dean swore at Simon and then stormed back up the driveway. We watched from the front room window as he climbed on his quad bike, revved the engine and raced away.

'Fuck,' I hissed, 'that was-'

'Leaflets!' Yasmin leaped on the settee, snatched the abortion leaflets and stuffed them into the front pocket of her hoodie as Simon came in saying

'I told you he was trouble, Yasmin.'

She had laid herself out on the settee, as though the whole event had only been a mere inconvenience. 'He was fine at the time, he'll get over it when he finds someone else to fuck.' I could see her using her hand to bury the leaflets deeper into her pockets.

'Don't use that sort of language with me.'

And they erupted into an argument as though I wasn't there. I remember standing there like a fucking idiot wishing I'd done something. After five minutes I left on the pretense that Mum had texted me.

I'm really worried what Dean will do to me at school tomorrow.

Henry (Admin1)

Tuesday, 20 February, 18:27.
Empty Nights

Yasmin called me last night, through the window. I was sitting at my desk writing the above post when I heard her.

She was leaning out of her window, her hands funneling her mouth. She was still wearing her hoodie.

'Yeah?' I asked.

'Louder.'

'What is it?'

'What?'

'What. Do. You. Want?'

Yasmin bellowed back an answer but the roar of a passing goods train drowned out her words. She picked up a sheet of paper and held it out her window. I recognised it as the volcanic rock essay for our geography coursework.

'What do you want to know?' I asked.

Yasmin glanced at the paper. 'How do I answer the first question?'

Mum shouted from her room so I turned my light out, dived into bed and texted Yasmin.

Me: I'll meet you on the footbridge in 20 minutes?

Yasmin: K.

I gave Mum ten minutes to fall back asleep before turning on my laptop and saving my coursework notes on a USB stick. Wilfred stirred as I closed the front door but didn't wake. I sprinted down the road to the footbridge and bounded up the steps as another goods trains roared passed in the opposite direction.

As the sound of the train faded away, the world became an unbroken and absolute silence. The motorway was too far away to hear, there were no birds or foxes or anything like that. You could see most of the town from the footbridge bathed in different shades of light. Yellow street lights illuminated the high street, red brake lights of cars on the distant motorway, The Shard was like a golden beacon in the far distance, the school field on the other side of town was masked by an inky blackness. I was reminded of a toy town a child would build and then leave in a darkened room.

I waited on the bridge for an unmeasurable amount of time, my hands resting against the metal handrail, the cold giving me goosebumps. Did you know that the stars in the sky are actually dead but it takes the light of those stars millions of years to reach earth?

I felt insignificant thinking about that. How many people are there are in the world and how did they get through life without knowing what was going to happen next? What did they do? What did the people in the luxury flats by the river do? What should I do?

Metallic footfalls intruded on the silence. Yasmin had removed her makeup but had zipped up her hoodie, her hands buried deep in its pockets. In the moonlight, I could see the faded logo across her chest.

'Hey,' she said. I watched her breath turn to mist in the night air.

I gave her my USB stick. 'Those are just my notes but they'll help.'

'Cheers, Hen.' She lit up a cigarette.

I could see she was pregnant now. There was a visible bump where the thing that would one day be alive was growing.

Yasmin allowed the smoke to escape her lips and said, 'its quiet tonight, isn't it?'

I slept through all my alarms and Mum woke me up, stressing that I was going to be late. I missed the bus to school so when I reached tutor Mr Sandil was half way through his announcements.

'Mrs Barton has said that all your free periods are now cancelled until you have each given in your personal statements. Everyone with a free period this morning needs to meet Mrs Barton in Common Room. She also wants everyone to research universities because she feels this isn't being done.'

I swore. I had planned to hide in my IT room and sleep until English.

'We haven't had time,' Joe whined.

'I'm sorry but that's why Mrs Barton has said. She is willing to lead a lesson in today's first two periods for those who need help.'

Most of my tutor group went to the Common Room. Yasmin, Megan, Dean and twenty students from other tutor groups arrived five minutes later. Yasmin gave me a sly smile when she arrived but Dean blanked me. Mrs Barton told us to sit at the desks in the middle of the room and not to touch the computers.

'These years are some of the most important years in your life,' she started. I zoned out at that point. We'd all heard this speech countless times. I wasn't the only one disinterested. Yasmin and Megan were on their phones in the back row. Joe was doodling in his notebook. Even Adam and Grace looked vacant. After Mrs Barton had wasted fifteen minutes of our time talking about how scary the world was, she told us we could either look at job sites together, complete our statements or look at universities. I don't know why we couldn't do our own thing but the class voted for job sites first. Mrs Barton loaded the Government recommended website she wanted us to use.

'This test has been created by professionals. By answering the questions, you will find your career path. It's not something you would find on Facebook,' she insisted as we loaded personality tests. Except it was something you would find on Facebook. At the end of the first paragraph there was a smiley emoji.

It was basically twenty questions to see which job was the ideal job for you. I fail to see how a quiz can predict my future by only knowing twenty things about me. I filled out the questions as best as I could but I saw Dean clicking the first answer he saw.

'I'm meant to be a teacher,' I said to Adam. 'How about you?'

'Politician, Joe?'

'Firefighter apparently.'

Grace laughed when the test told her that her destiny was to be a team manager in retail and was then shouted at by Mrs Barton for not taking the quiz seriously.

Next we were given a list of universities in England to look at next. They all looked similar. Happy, grinning multicultural students smiling on sunny fields or standing in front of modern buildings. There were tons of degrees to choose from, degrees I didn't even know existed. I don't understand how we're qualified to do things like archaeology or philosophy. It was stupid looking at things we couldn't possibly obtain and we only had our predicted results to work from. I felt like shit reading some of the universities' websites. It wasn't what they said but how they phrased it.

Only students who have achieved three A's and one B in their A Level examinations will be considered for this course...

'It's not all about grades though,' Bethany Holder, a girl from my general studies class, shouted out, 'It's not all about results. What about location?'

'Yes, you need to look at location as well,' Mrs Barton said, 'If you want to move out from home, you need to look at what accommodation the university provides and after your first year-'

But everyone was talking about moving out.

'I wanna move out,' Joe said, 'It'll be bloody brilliant.'

'I dunno,' I muttered.

'C'mon,' Joe said, 'you can come and go whenever you want, make new friends, take girls home...'

'What about your flat mates?' I said, 'you can't choose them. What if you get stuck with complete bastards for a year?'

Joe admitted he hadn't thought about this but assured us it wouldn't be a problem.

I don't want to move out. I can see the appeal of it, though. You can go to parties, do whatever you want but rent prices and accommodation costs are ridiculous. The biggest issue for me would be leaving Mum and Wilfred. It would break Mum's heart if I left. No matter how often Joe kept saying it would be like the films, I doubted it would be.

'This one charges an application fee just to apply to them,' Adam said, pointing to his screen.

Mrs Barton peered over Adam's shoulder and started to talk about tuition fees and how much we were entitled to.

The class then argued over whose fault our student loans are. I didn't take part because in our school the person who wins the argument is normally the one who shouts the loudest.

I completed my personal statement at the end of the lesson. It's shit, I've done eight drafts of it but I don't know what else to write.

Henry (Admin1)

Tuesday, 20 February, 20:23.
Dean

I struggled to stay awake through general studies and at lunch I went to the IT room so I could doze. Adam was writing up his notes about a prefect meeting he went to last week, Joe was on YouTube. The classroom door flew open and a crowd of year sevens poured in led by Dean. I was too stunned to do anything. Joe jumped up but Dean pushed him back into his seat and held him there. The year sevens emptied our bags onto the floor, flipped over the tables and chairs and scrambled under desks to unplug our computers. Joe tried to slap them aside but there were too many of them to control.

A teacher, investigating the noise, ordered everyone out of the classroom. Adam, showing the teacher his prefect badge, convinced her that we should stay but in return we had to clean up the mess and write an incident form. An incident form all three of us knew would be filed away and forgotten.

'Arseholes,' Joe bellowed when the teacher was out of earshot.

'We'll be late to our last lesson,' Adam complained. He threw an empty coke can into the bin but it bounced off the rim. 'Fuck sake.'

'Why don't you tell Mrs Barton to expel Dean or exclude him or something?' Joe said.

'No point. He won't be kicked out this close to the exams.'

Adam had a point, Mrs Barton wouldn't exclude anyone now. I'm honestly surprised Dean didn't beat me up or do something worse. Maybe he will later.

'Doesn't matter. All he's gonna be is a druggy on the streets or somethin,' ain't he?' Joe said.

I laughed but Joe kept talking.

'This will be the highlight of his life, don't you think? The final year. Then that's it for him but we... we have plans don't we?'

Joe looked between me and Adam pleading for us to agree with him. 'We have plans. Like, what we're gonna do after Uni.'

'I'll probably be working in an office in London,' Adam shrugged, 'Working my way up to be a team leader or something.'

'Exactly. Henry, what will you be?'

I didn't know what to say, luckily Joe answered his own question.

'A teacher. Hen, you would be a fantastic teacher.'

He must of been thinking about the online quiz. I would hate being a teacher. Teaching kids like Dean all day? I didn't say anything, though.

'I could be a…a…' Joe stumbled.

'Game tester?' Adam suggested.

'You could work as a Game Developer and do a course on it at Uni,' I said.

'Exactly. I'd like it there,' Joe grinned. While Joe always achieved A Stars in his IT classes I doubted he would be able to code a game. We humoured him for a while by suggesting what jobs games he would make as we cleaned up the computer room.

When the bell went, Adam left first because he was most concerned about his attendance. Joe and I didn't care if we were five or ten minutes late. I walked with Joe as far as reception, talking about the future.

'It's scary shit, man,' Joe kept saying.

'It'll be fine. I mean, things always are, aren't they?' I hope I sounded more confident than I felt.

I had to go to my history lesson which was at the opposite end of the school to Joe's maths class. We separated at reception and I told him I would see him tomorrow in tutor time. As I walked away I heard the reception door buzz open.

Joe has bunked tons of lessons before but I wanted to check if he was alright. I peered through the reception window. Joe was walking through the school car park towards the bus stop. I couldn't be sure but I think he was shaking.

I thought about telling Mrs Barton about Dean but she wouldn't do anything. Even if she did Dean would retaliate. I sat through the history lesson in silence and gave in my latest essay knowing it was only worth a D.

After my driving lesson that evening I played with Joe on the Xbox and he seemed a bit happier.

Henry (Admin1)

Thursday, 22 February 22:34.
My Birthday

Today is my seventeenth birthday. Mum woke me up five minutes earlier so I could open my presents before breakfast. She'd bought me a game for my Xbox and a poster for my bedroom wall. Dad brought me a new headset for when I play online with Joe and Adam. Uncle Patrick gave me fifty pounds in a card. Wilfred bounded around the room, leaping through the discarded wrapping paper.

I checked my Facebook Wall during tutor time when Mr Sandil was going through the morning announcements.

'Mrs Barton has organised a Sixth form trip to Stanlow University. They are having an open day where reps from other universities will be there to tell you about student life.' Mr Sandil gave us a letter about the trips for our parents, I stuffed mine in my bag and continued to scroll through my Facebook wall. I had twenty seven birthday messages.

I was on my way to my English lesson when Dad rang me.

'Happy Birthday, Hen.'

'Cheers, Dad. I'm at school.'

'Alright, I'll ring you later on. Did you like headset I got you? Was it the right one?'

'Yeah, yeah it was great.'

It took me ten minutes to get Dad off the phone. Then Grace stopped me in the English corridor before I could reach Mrs Hughes' classroom.

'Happy Birthday,' she said to me and gave me this awkward hug. I swear, Grace has no concept of personal space. I had to tell Grace I was late to class to make her leave.

Mrs Hughes returned my Gatsby essay, I scored a B, my highest mark so far. She also wished me happy birthday. When I checked my Facebook at break time I had fifty four messages. The two hour history lesson that followed resulted in another essay being set for homework. Mrs Barton returned my essay. Another D.

I phoned Dad back at lunch but he didn't answer. I phoned Mum afterwards and she said Patrick had booked a table at the Harvester for tonight.

'I can't believe I got a D in history,' I said to Grace in geography. 'I didn't deserve that.' Mrs Barton had said to me that my history grades had been dropping. It's true, they have but I have more important things to worry about, don't I?

'Yeah. Mrs Barton is a total bitch.'

'Deserving isn't how the world works,' Mr Roth said. 'Did I hear that right, today's your birthday Henry?'

'Yes it is,' Grace squealed.

Mr Roth said that he didn't like to think about his birthdays anymore because he thought they were depressing. We didn't do anything in that lesson. We just chatted. As the bell rang for the end of the lesson Mr Roth asked 'has anyone seen Yasmin recently?' He looked right at me but I didn't say anything.

I spotted Yasmin at her window before I left for the Harvester. She waved and sent me a text a few minutes later.

Yasmin: Happy Birthday!

Henry (Admin1)

Saturday, 24 February, 21:01
Linda

Dad picked me up from the house this morning so we could watch a film together in town. Dad said it was my birthday treat from him despite the fact he'd already brought me a headset. Afterwards we had a steak and chips and Dad wanted to know when I was going to book my driving test and what sort of car I wanted to buy. I told him I didn't know. He was telling me about the rules of the motorway on the way home when his phone rang.

'Hello?'

I could hear a female voice at the other end but I couldn't hear what was being said.

'Now? Hold on.'

The car swerved as Dad lowered the phone. 'Henry, how do you fancy meeting Linda? I've got to nip back to the house for a minute to pick something up. You okay with that?'

'Yeah.'

Dad put the phone back to his ear, 'We're on our way.'

Linda's front garden was made of plastic. Fake grass had been laid by the door and still held pieces of mud and dirt. Plants had been placed around the edges of the garden but they looked too shiny and clean to have been real. As we pulled up I saw plastic windmills spin in the flower beds and an upstairs curtain twitch. Dad texted Linda that we were outside.

A woman a few years younger than Mum jogged out of a house towards the car. 'Hey,' she purred and gave Dad a peck on the cheek. She was wearing a tracksuit and had white headphones wires snaking up under her shirt. 'Are you Henry? It's lovely to meet you.' Her voice had a slight accent but I couldn't place it. She handed Dad an envelope and asked him to take it to the solicitors after he had dropped me off.

Henry (Admin1)

Monday, 26 February, 17:43.

Tact

The school day is nine till three but most of the time we finish at four because we have revision classes. Normally whoever teaches us for period five keeps us behind for an extra class but sometimes your other teachers come and find you and argue over which revision class you should be in. It's bloody hilarious when it happens.

My final lesson today was geography.

'I didn't put a page number on this one,' Grace said, screwing up a page. I double checked my own papers numbers. I know Yasmin is half way through her coursework, she told me that she is going to do an all nighter to catch up. Dean isn't in class today. I don't think he's even started his.

'I'm missing a couple of pages,' I said.

'What ones?' Grace asked.

'Pages six and seven. I think it's the only thing I need, then I'm done.'

'Do you want me to print it off for you, Hen? I'm going to the printer now.'

'No it's okay, I need to finish proofreading the rest of it.'

'Are you sure? It'll only take a second. I'm going that way anyway.'

'No, it's fine. Do you have a stapler?'

As Grace bounded towards Mr Roth's desk, the door opened. Mrs Barton stood in the doorway. Grace skidded to a halt almost colliding with her.

'Henry, Will, Grace and Bobbie. I want you in my revision class.' She ignored Mr Roth who was standing literally next to her.

Mr Roth smiled at her. 'Mrs Barton, how can I help?'

'I want Henry, Will, Grace and Bobbie in my revision class,' Mrs Barton repeated but the confidence in her voice had faded.

Grace scampered back to her desk, clutching Mr Roth's stapler.

'I'm afraid they're in my revision class to complete their coursework,' Mr Roth said. 'Maybe you could take them another day?'

'No. I need them today. Today is the only day I have free to teach them.' She turned to us. 'Come on.'

No one moved.

'Maybe they can start your revision classes when they finish mine? This section of their coursework needs to be completed today. The deadline is in twenty minutes.'

Mrs Barton's mouth opened and closed, her brain struggling to form an argument to such a reasonable request. 'Ok. Yeah, okay that's fine. Yeah that's fine.'

When she closed the classroom door Mr Roth stuck out his tongue.

'That's another skill you'll all need for adult life. Tact,' he said, 'the ability to tell someone to go to hell in such a way that they look forward to the trip.'

It's good to know that the other teachers don't like Mrs Barton either.

Henry (Admin1)

Wednesday, 28 February, 19:39.

Roundabouts

I hate roundabouts. I understand what I'm meant to do but either I'm in the wrong lane or the other drivers are going too fast. Colin and I practiced at a roundabout at the far end of the high street. The turning we wanted, towards Asda was only two lanes wide. I panicked the first time and took the wrong exit, without signaling. Someone blasted their horn and Colin snatched the wheel. He pulled me over and we discussed what went wrong.

On my second attempt I drifted into the wrong lane but there was no traffic to crash into. On the third attempt I pulled out of my lane too soon and another car skidded to avoid me.

Colin drove me home but told me not to worry about it and that we would work on it in the next lesson.

Henry (Admin1)

Thursday, 1 March, 21:43

Spain

I was getting changed out of my sixth form suit and into jeans so I could go cinema with Dad when I heard the doorbell go. I raced onto the landing but instead of Dad I heard Uncle Patrick.

'What're you doing? Paul'll be here in a minute,' Mum said.

'You shouldn't be talking to him, Carol.'

I was about to go back into my room when I heard Mum say, 'I won't have to for much longer, will I? He's moving.'

'Where?' I heard Uncle Patrick asked.

'Spain. With Linda.'

Spain?

Despite Mum's pleading Uncle Patrick refused to speak to Dad.

'Hey, buddy? You okay?' Dad asked me when I got into his car.

'Yeah. I'm good, let's go.'

Dad brought me home at nine. He didn't mention moving to Spain.

Henry (Admin1)

Friday, 2 March, 17:01.

Day off school

Mum told me that there was a planned teacher strike today and that I should have known about it because it had been all over the news. I think Mr Sandil mentioned it in tutor time the other day but I was googling abortion stuff at the time. The teachers were striking over pay so all the students in England have the day off school. It's interesting to see the reaction to this on Facebook.

Chelsea: OMG. Day off school because of stupid teacher strike. Going to the park with my ladies in the sun. #blessed.

Some of the students like Adam were actually arguing for the teachers.

Adam: Teachers should have equal pay for the tireless work they do.

He then posted a link to a BBC article about the strike. I don't have an opinion on it. The strike doesn't concern me, all I know is that it has given me a day off school. I know I should have done revision but I felt Yasmin was more important. I texted her:

Me: Do you want me to come over today and do more research?

Yasmin: Can't I'm busy. Soz.

Before I put my phone down Joe texted me.

Joe: You want to go cinema today?

Me: Cool.

I told Mum I was going to watch a film in town with Joe. She asked me why I didn't ask if Dad wanted to meet up instead. I told her I didn't want to. Mum just said 'ok' and curled back up on the settee with Wilfred.

When I got home that evening Mum was asleep on the settee, Wilfred was still on her lap. I don't think either of them had moved all day. I crept upstairs and turned on my laptop. The first thing I saw on my Facebook feed was that Yasmin had been tagged in a picture. She was sitting in the park with Chelsey, Megan and Jake pouting at the camera.

That really pissed me off so I've written this post to distract myself.

Henry (Admin1)

Saturday, 3 March, 15:02.

Roundabouts again

I. Fucking. Hate. Roundabouts.

Henry (Admin1)

Saturday, 3 March, 18:39.

CV dropping along the high street

I'm meant to have been job hunting these past couple of weeks but I think it's pointless. Let's say I get a job tomorrow, I'd only be able to keep it until my A Levels then I'll have to leave to do revision. Mum says that they can't fire you if you take time off to revise for exams but I heard that they can.

Mum and I printed off my CV and we went up the high street dropping them off into shops. We printed off twenty copies but we could only give away two. Even though some of the shops are small businesses they wouldn't take CV's. They all said to apply online.

We had a Chinese afterwards to cheer ourselves up.

Henry (Admin1)

Sunday, 4 March, 19:35.

Applying online

I don't want to write about job hunting because it's depressing but Doctor West said I should. Mum and I are going to look at job websites every other night. Some of the applications are really easy. You click apply, click attach CV and then submit. Others you have to fill in these long forms that take hours. Mum is looking for a job too. Now Dad has left she says we need more income.

Henry (Admin1)

Monday, 5 March, 21:29.

Money

I've been thinking a lot about money. I was looking up student loans, grants and how much student accommodation costs. Even after their first year in halls, students have to find their own homes and the closer to a city you are the more expensive it is. I read online that students hardly ever pay back their student loans and some die in debt. I realised how bad our money situation is when Uncle Patrick popped round unexpectedly. I was doing my general studies coursework and Mum was paying the bills. She keeps a record of all the bills she's received in the post and had the paperwork across the front room floor when the doorbell rang. I heard her answer the door and I heard Uncle Patrick saying, 'Five seven. We beat them five seven.'

He was talking about the local football, Mum called me downstairs and lead Uncle Patrick into the kitchen. As Uncle Patrick was explaining that he had come over to pick up a phone charger he had left behind from when he was stopping over, Mum hissed in my ear

'Pick up all the papers on the floor and put them in my room. Now.'

I took the papers upstairs while Mum distracted Uncle Patrick by making him a cup of tea and asking about the football. I didn't understand most of what I read but I saw lots of negative numbers typed in red.

When I tried to speak about it to Mum after Uncle Patrick had left she refused to answer my questions so it must be pretty bad.

Henry (Admin1)

Wednesday, 7 March, 12:01.

School legends

A school legend is something that happened at school and every time the story is told it changes until no one knows what actually happened. Like Chinese whispers.

I woke up before the Cannon Street train this morning and caught an earlier bus to school. When I arrived I decided to work on my geography coursework in the Common Room for a change. Will, a boy from my general studies class, was laying out on one of the settees, flanked by two friends.

'You alright?' I asked.

Will's response was a moan.

'He's hungover,' Bethany Holder said. 'We went to a party last night and it finished at five. We were here at seven for the breakfast club in the canteen.'

I'm not invited to these sort of parties. I know I wouldn't enjoy them but I'd like to be invited anyway.

Will heaved. I took a step back as Will's friend picked up a bin and placed it before him.

'If Mrs Barton sees him, she'll kick him out,' Bethany whispered.

As more people came into the Common Room Will got worse. I left when the bell went for tutor time and told Joe and Adam what I'd seen.

'Legend,' Joe smirked. 'I remember my first time I got hammered. I had a fight on the night bus on the way home.'

'I don't think it's Will's first time drinking,' Adam said.

'Oh. He's a lightweight then.'

I had a meeting with Mrs Saunders that day but I didn't tell her about Will.

We spoke about my coursework and the grades I was getting and where I could improve. As we were planning my next appointment she asked how I felt about our meetings.

'I like them,' I said. 'It makes everything clearer, y'know?'

'And you can tell me anything, can't you Henry? You realise that, don't you?'

'Yeah, I know.'

I still didn't tell her about Will.

Adam told me what happened to Will that evening on the Xbox as we played Grand Theft Auto. Will had his first two lessons free and his music teacher for his third and fourth lesson let him to sleep at the back of the class. Mrs Barton overheard some students talking about him in the corridor but when she cornered Will after school he was sober enough to talk his way out of trouble.

Then Joe came online and we played a versus match on Call of Duty.

'Hen, stop perving on Yasmin through your window and cover me,' Joe said as I died for the twelfth time that match.

'Piss off,' I said but he was right, I had been watching Yasmin through her window. She was in her pajamas talking on her phone. I wondered if she wanted me or wanted to speak to me but she closed her curtains and I returned to my game.

Henry (Admin1)

Friday, 9 March, 20:58.

I have a Job interview

I have a job interview at Aglet, a new shoe shop on the high street. I did an email application with Mum last week and they sent me a reply this afternoon. Mum googled the company and told me their history all the way back to 1935.

'I won't need to know this.'

'Yes you will. It's a job interview Henry, they expect all applicants to know about the company.'

There is a difference between knowing about the company and knowing the history of the company. Dad agreed with me too, he wished me best of luck for the interview when we went cinema this evening but told me not to worry too much about it because it wasn't a proper job.

The interview is on Wednesday.

Henry (Admin1)

Wednesday, 16 March, 20:24

Aglet Job interview.

The interview was in the local job centre. Mum dropped me off and reminded me to offer them my CV which I took with me in a folder.

'I have an interview with Aglet,' I told one of the security guards.

I was directed to a row of seats placed opposite a glass booth at the far end of the first floor. Every ten minutes the interviewer would come out of the booth with an interviewee and take in the next candidate. There were five of us waiting to be called in. We each looked nervous but I must have looked the most awkward. I was the only one wearing a suit.

The people in the job centre made me think of what Yasmin and Dean would be like in the future. One boy who must have been three years older than me was screaming at his career advisor because she wouldn't grant him his benefits. Security had to remove him from building. The boy's shouts set off two babies in a double pram who screeched until their mother, a few years older than Yasmin, was asked to leave the room.

After ten minutes of waiting, the interviewer emerged from the booth and called my name.

'Hello, Henry. My name is Michael, I represent The Aglet Company. Today we're interviewing for the position of sales assistant. Before we start, can I offer you a glass of water?' It sounded as though he was speaking from a rehearsed script.

Michael asked what I knew about the company and I told him what I'd read on the company's Wikipedia page. When I finished, he nodded and then explained what was expected in the job.

'Do you want to see my CV?' I asked when he had finished.

Michael scanned it then passed it back. 'Why did you apply for the role?' he asked.

The correct answer was "money" and "my mum told me to" but I said I wanted to take a job so I could help my mother out at home and learn more about the world. It's a really cheesy answer but it was all I could think of.

'What's the capital of England?' Michael asked.

'I'm sorry?'

'Can you tell me what the capital of England is, please?'

Mum said they throw in these really random questions sometimes to see how you think. How many ping pong balls can you fit inside a limo? What superpower would you have?

Then he asked normal interview questions. Give me an example of when you were a team player, an example of leadership, an example of when you went beyond your job description to help somebody. I could see his eyes looking past me out the window at the queue of other interviewees and I figured there were so many of them I didn't stand a chance.

Mum quizzed me about the interview as soon as I got in the car to go home. 'How did it go?'

'Fine. I think it went well.'

'Did you offer him your CV?'

'Yeah.'

'Did he take it?'

'He looked at it.'

'He looked at it,' Mum repeated. Then she asked me what answers I'd given. I could tell she didn't approve of what I had said but she didn't say anything about it.

Henry (Admin1)

Monday, 19 March, 12:38.
Joe's driving test

Joe was talking about his driving test in tutor. Apparently he had to book it in the middle of the school day, during English but if Mrs Hughes had known I doubted she would have minded.

'I failed my first, had too many minors and I'm waiting to pick a date for the second test,' Adam told us but I doubted Joe heard him.

'Did you know that the sooner you pass the test, the better driver you are?' Joe said.

I thought that the exact opposite was true.

I'd been avoiding the driving books Mum had brought me. I've got other problems.

English was cancelled because Mrs Hughes was off sick so I spent the free hours researching abortion stories in the IT room. Adam was in the room with me but I had my screen tilted away from him.

'You really hanging around with Yasmin, then?' he asked me.

'Yeah, we live opposite each other.'

'You friends?'

I closed down the website I was viewing, a forum for teenage mothers. 'Yeah, we went to the same primary school.'

'Right,' Adam said. 'I don't really speak to her. She decent?'

'Yeah,' I said. 'She's alright.'

'I've seen who she hangs around with,' Adam said but then changed the subject and started talking about his drama coursework. I reopened the website and continued to read.

We found Joe in the canteen at lunchtime.

'How'd it go?' Adam asked.

'The bastard examiner failed me for speeding.' Joe's eyes were red as though he had been crying and had been trying to hide it.

'How come?' I asked.

'You know Perkin's Lane?'

'Yeah.'

'Well they're doing the road up there but they started work last night. The workmen put up these twenty miles per hour signs, y'know? Like lollypop signs only the wind knocked them over, didn't it? It's meant to be thirty on that road,' Joe hissed,' but the examiner did an emergency stop because he thought I was driving too fuckin' fast. Prick.' Joe stabbed his jacket potato so hard that his plastic fork snapped in half.

'How many minors and majors did they give you?'

'Literally just that one major. I would have fuckin' passed otherwise.'

Henry (Admin1)

Tuesday, 20 March, 23:01.

Visiting Stanlow University

Mum found the letter about Stanlow University yesterday and insisted I go. She then went on a rant about why I didn't tell her, she's been really stressed recently, with finding a job, worrying about my grades and Dad leaving so I agreed to go just to keep her happy.

The trip was led by Mrs Barton. Luckily Adam was coming too and it meant missing double history.

On the coach to Stanlow University, Adam and I were talking about university life. 'Joe keeps saying that in dorms it's a total orgy,' Adam said, 'You get girls come in from other countries, guys too, with different accents and different views on life. They come from all different cultures.'

'Yeah they let anyone into Stanlow,' I said. 'If not through results than at least through clearing.'

I could see that Adam really wanted to talk about girls and the chances of finding a girlfriend at university. The only one of us to have a girlfriend before was Joe but that was in year ten for a week I don't know if that counts. I'd been thinking about what Yasmin would be like at University and what the other girls there would be like but I didn't know how to say this to Adam so we stopped talking about it.

When Adam goes to Uni, if he does go, he won't have a problem finding a girlfriend. I know some of the girls at school fancy him. Joe is charismatic enough not to have a problem either.

Mrs Barton tried to convince us that Stanlow University was really prestigious. She was trying to scare us into doing revision but as we approached the university I saw a group of students smoking by the front gate and it looked like Norcrest, only bigger. We were ushered into a hall which was twice the size of our canteen. There were rows of stalls from different universities, manned by three representatives.

'You have three hours before we meet back at the coach,' Mrs Barton said, 'collect as many leaflets and prospectuses as you can and remember you are representing the school.'

There were other Sixth forms attending and I soon lost Adam in the crowd. There were so many stall owners shouting, so many beckoning potential students over with promises of offers and deals that it felt like a marketplace. I was pressured into signing an emailing list for five different university clubs. That's the thing about university, there're are hundreds of clubs. Doctor Who Club, Sherlock Club, Basketball Club, Harry Potter Appreciation Club, Fencing Club, Dueling Cub, Archery Club, Cosplay Club, Rowing Club, Swimming Club. Those are some of the ones I can remember.

I took a tour around campus with five other Sixth form students and a current Stanlow student called Milo. Milo explained she was from Mexico and she was doing a degree to become a fitness coach which would take her three years. She showed us the main hall, the canteens, several cafes and then a lecture hall. I don't know how to describe a lecture hall. I suppose it's like a church but with the rows of seats higher so everyone can see the front.

Then Milo took us to the dorms, I didn't like them. Milo said there are several halls available and within them several different types of rooms. You could have a shared bathroom but I really wouldn't like sharing my bathroom with strangers. I mean, what about taking a shower and using the loo? I was even more put off when Milo explained that the doors didn't have any locks and that some students brought their own locks from home. The first room we went into had been cleaned but our group struggled to fit inside. I was reminded of a shoebox. The next room we were shown had an ensuite but it was more like a cupboard and the shower door didn't fully cover you.

As we were leaving on the coach we saw a girl crying and shouting at her friends by the University gates. She threw her backpack at them, the zip broke and the papers inside blew away in the wind. The girl then collapsed on the pavement, crying and her friends darted among the traffic collecting her belongings. Everyone was watching them.

I hope I never get that stressed.

On the trip back, Adam and I flicked through the prospectuses we had collected.

'Have you seen the reading lists for the English courses?' Adam asked me.

I had. The list was two pages long and I only recognised five of the titles.

'Yeah. Bloody hell, they do a course on… architectural technology. What's that, different tools used to build stuff?'

'Why would they do a course on that?' Adam asked.

I shrugged and found another interesting course, 'Game cultures,'

'That's not what you think,' Adam said, 'it's not making games.'

I finished reading through all the prospectus I collected at home but I couldn't find a course that interests me.

Henry (Admin1)

Wednesday, 21 March, 19:55.

Planning Parent's Evening

'There's going to be a Sixth form parents evening next Monday,' Mr Sandil said in tutor time this morning.

'Why's it so soon?' Joe asked 'Why weren't we told last week?'

'The admin department made a mistake and it's happening next week Monday. I'm sorry but that's the way it is.'

'What's the point? We've only got a few weeks left,' Joe said but Mr Sandil ignored him.

We would have to book a ten minute slot with each of our teachers so they could discuss how we were doing with our parents. Some schools stop doing parent's evenings after year eleven but Norcrest was one of the few that didn't. They're a complete waste of time.

When I got home I told Mum about the parent's evening. 'What about Dad?' I asked. Mum and Dad were on speaking terms but having them spending an evening together was questionable. The most time they had spent together since the breakup was when Dad had picked up his stuff from the house. Mum hesitated and said if I wanted Dad there I should invite him.

When Dad answered my call there was cheering in the background. It sounded like he was in the pub watching football.

'Hey Dad. How's things?'

'Yeah good. Everything alright?'

'Yeah fine, I've got a parents evening coming up.'

'Hold on,' the sounds of the football game faded away. 'What was that?'

'I've got a parent's evening coming up, in three weeks' time. Do you wanna come?'

'Yeah, with you and your mum?'

'Yeah.'

'Course. What time and when?'

I told him the details over the phone and he agreed to meet us outside the school.

Henry (Admin1)

Friday, 23 March, 19:01.

The Rebound

Yasmin texted me this morning and asked if I wanted to come over. I can't remember the last time I saw her in geography or smoking in Jake's car.

My third and fourth periods were free so I caught the bus back to my house and walked over the footbridge.

When Yasmin opened the front door my eyes were drawn to her belly. There was a visible bump but it could pass for belly fat.

'I know,' she said.

'Has your dad noticed?'

'Dad thinks I've had lots of Big Macs. Let's keep it that way.'

I could only see that decision ending horribly.

'How was the school trip to Stanlow?' she asked.

'I got tons of prospectuses to look through. Do you want them when I've finished?'

'Nah, I'm fine.'

'What are you thinking of doing when Sixth form is over?' Going to Uni?' I could see Yasmin living the student lifestyle, partying every night. She'd like that.

'Dunno.'

'Any word from Dean?'

'No.'

I didn't tell Yasmin that Dean attacked me in the IT room. 'I've not seen him at school in a while, either,' I added but Yasmin only grunted.

Yasmin explained that her Dad was at a meeting in London with a potential client so we started doing more research into the Mistveil clinic. We found a list of their staff and googled each of them in turn, as well as looking at the clinics' reviews online. I could tell Yasmin had already done this, she knew what links to click on and what websites to go to. It was like I was a teacher and Yasmin wanted impress me with her homework.

'Are you sure you want to go here?' I asked as we returned to the Mistveil Clinic's homepage.

'Yeah.'

'Have you been there before?'

'Course not.'

'Then you should go there,' I said 'and scout out the area.'

'What?'

'Go in, pick up some leaflets, talk to them and look around.'

Dad does these things called dummy runs. If he needed to go somewhere he hadn't been before he would drive there and back a few days before so he knew where he was going. Ironically Dad was doing a dummy run to the hospital when Mum went into labour at home and I was born. I thought it would be a good idea to do a dummy run to Mistveil Clinic with Yasmin so she knew how long the route would take on the bus.

Mistveil looked alright. The walls were pebble dashed and in front of the building was a car park with five parking spots. When Yasmin asked me what I thought it was like inside I peeked through the window.

'It's like a dentist's waiting room,' I told her. Plastic chairs had been set around the room and a pile of magazines had been placed on a coffee table. A sign on the door read: Closed for lunch.

We'd just got back to Yasmin's house when it happened. I was asking if the doctors were allowed to perform the operation without a parent's permission when Yasmin's phone vibrated. She looked at the screen, gave a cry and flung it across the room.

'Yasmin?'

She ran upstairs and slammed the door.

It took me a minute to realise that it wasn't my anything I'd said. When I picked up the phone I saw, through the already cracked screen, a selfie taken by Dean and another girl. Judging from the sheets on their chests, they were in bed.

I called up the stairs but Yasmin didn't come down. I tried saying things I had heard other girls at school say like 'you're better off without him,' but the only response was a very weak,

'Piss off.'

I didn't know what else to do so I left.

Henry (Admin1)

Sunday, 25 March, 12:32.

Mum's got a Job

I haven't spoken to Yasmin since she received the selfie of Dean and his new girlfriend. I know Yasmin's alright though. I've glimpsed her through the window this morning and she's still active on Facebook. She posted a passive aggressive status yesterday.

Yasmin: I'm feeling so betrayed. People are nothing but trouble. I should have learned by now.

It has over fifty comments most of which are by Megan and Chelsea. They'll be much better at comforting Yasmin than I was. I'm glad Yasmin and Dean have broken up if I'm honest.

I do have some good news, Mum's got a job. She knows a friend of a friend who left their job at the dry cleaners on the high street. Mum went into the shop, explained she knew the person who was leaving and then they called her back that afternoon and asked if she could start Monday. It means Mum will be out the house more often so I can spend more time researching abortions and revising before my A levels.

Henry (Admin1)

Monday, 26 March, 23:24.

Parent's evening

On the night of the parent's evening I stayed in the IT room watching abortion documentaries. I found a video that was a recording of an abortion procedure but I had to turn it off after two minutes. I was glad when Mum texted me that she was outside.

'Hey Henry,' Mum said and gave me a hug. Dad was already there and gave me a wide smile.

'Are you ready to go in?' I asked.

There was a silence in which Mum and Dad shared a glance. I sensed I had interrupted their conversation. A conversation about Spain, no doubt.

'Did Mum tell you about her new job?' I asked as I walked them towards reception.

'Oh, it is any good?' Dad asked

'It's nothing, dry cleaners,' Mum muttered.

Chairs had been placed in the middle of the assembly hall so you could wait until a teacher called you over. I'd arranged time slots but everyone jumps the queue. As we entered the hall Mr Roth called us over.

'I love these evenings,' Mr Roth admitted as we sat down, 'so I can shout at students' parents.'

He explained to Mum and Dad that compared to my scores at the start of the year I was improving. He had all of my coursework there and showed me how my grade had risen from a D to a B. When he explained that my predicted coursework grade was an A star Mum was beaming.

'My only criticism would be not to become distracted talking to other students but apart from that everything is fine. I have no worries,' Mr Roth said.

I thought that was brilliant feedback but as we left so Mr Roth could see Adam and his parents Mum said to me 'Henry, did you hear that? You mustn't talk in class so much. I can't believe it.'

You'd think I'd fucking shot someone.

We saw Mrs Hughes twenty minutes behind our scheduled time slot. 'What can I say about Henry? He's one of the worst students I've ever taught. Did you receive the letter I sent last week about him throwing chairs across the classroom?'

Mum laughed but Dad thought, for a microsecond, that she was serious. Mrs Hughes' feedback was that my essay answers were improving but I needed to complete some wider reading. She also reminded me that I had an essay about *Romeo and Juliet* due. My general studies teacher said everything was fine too. I spotted Grace and her Dad on the far side of the hall but before I could say anything to her Mrs Barton called us over.

'Hello, I'm Mrs Barton, Henry's history teacher and head of year,' she shook Mum and Dad's hand. 'Let's talk about Henry's grades,' Mrs Barton said. 'His essay quality is slipping.'

'Oh,' said Mum, 'I didn't ...realise.'

I swear, I could have punched Mrs Barton right there.

Mrs Barton took out my essays and laid them across the table, like a poker player revealing their hand. 'Henry's grade throughout the year has been a consistent D, he's failed to improve. He always appears disinterested in class.'

'I'm so sorry,' Mum said, 'Henry, did you hear that? I-'

'What are the class studying in history?' Dad asked reading the title of one of my papers.

Mrs Barton looked taken aback as though Dad had asked her what year it was. 'Germany and Italy. Before the First World War.'

Dad nodded.

'We have homework due for our lesson next week,' Mrs Barton added and I could see she was trying to hold back a smile. 'Explain the international factors that lead to the German Economic Crisis of 1890.'

'Oh yes, I'll make sure he does it. Henry, you must do that essay, okay? I'm so sorry,' Mum blathered.

The meeting continued for another minute but it was just Mum promising I would do better and Mrs Barton saying goodbye so she could see the next student.

'Why haven't you been doing your history homework?' Mum snapped at me as soon as we left the hall.

'I've had other things to do. More important things.'

'Henry, history is an A Level.'

'He's not learning anything useful in the class anyway, is he?' Dad said. 'I wouldn't worry about it, Hen.'

'That's not the point,' Mum shrieked, 'he needs the UCAS points to enter university.'

They argued all the way back to the school gates before Mum said she was tired. Dad said he had to leave and gave me a hug before walking to the bus stop. I think Dad argued with Mum just to get her off my back.

Henry (Admin1)

Tuesday, 27 March, 19:00
Near miss

I almost had another crash in my driving lesson this evening. I was driving along the A road that leads into town when a car swerved into the lane ahead of me. Colin shouted and slammed on his brake pedal. I blasted the horn as the other car shot off down the road.

'Wanker,' Colin muttered.

I was going to laugh at him for swearing but then a quad bike zoomed passed us. It weaved in and out of the lanes, chasing after the car.

'That's a boy from my school,' I said.

Dean disappeared from view and I recognised the car as Jake's.

'They'll both crash if they're not careful. Take the next exit and we'll come off there.'

I don't think Jake and Dean saw me. The rest of the lesson passed without incident.

Henry (Admin1)

Wednesday 28 March, 13:04.
Bunking off history

I missed the bus this morning. I was texting Yasmin, she's not answered any of my other texts, and left the house late. The bus driver saw me running but laughed and pulled away so I had to wait half an hour for the next bus and the time I reached the school I was twenty five minutes late for my history lesson. After parent's evening Mrs Barton would have gone mental if I came in late. Instead I went to the IT room to finish my essay on *Romeo and Juliet*.

I couldn't concentrate though. I kept thinking about Yasmin and how she thought that Dean sleeping with another girl was a world ending event when it really wasn't. I couldn't believe she was pregnant the dealing with it behind her Dad's back. I couldn't believe I was sitting there pretending to care about *Romeo and Juliet* when so many other more important things were happening around me. I started to practice the grounding exercises Dr West had taught in preparation for my exams. I closed my eyes and breathed in through my nose and out through my mouth for ten breaths. When that didn't work I tried again. Before I finished my third cycle a hand slapped my desk. I jumped.

'Henry, why aren't you in my class?'

Mrs Barton snarled like a rabid dog. I opened my mouth but no words came out. She was supposed to be in my history lesson at the other side of the school.

I tried to speak but no words came.

She scowled at my essay as though it had offended her, 'At least tell me that's history homework.' Her hand swooped across the desk and closed on my papers. 'You can finish this in detention.'

'Oi!' I snatched the papers as Mrs Barton turned away. The essay ripped in two, one half stayed in Mrs Barton's hand, the other half fluttered to the floor. I could've sworn I saw heard her scoff under her breath.

'You better give that fucking paper back to me.'

Mrs Barton blinked. 'What… did you just say?' she asked in a forced calmness.

'I said, you better that fucking paper back to me, Mrs Barton.'

I'm shit at arguing back but I could tell that she was on the cusp of losing it.

'Do you really want to fail your A Levels, Henry, and waste your life? Because that's what –'

'End up like you, you mean?'

Mrs Barton flinched.

'We can finish this conversation in detention,' she whispered in a voice that could have turned into a shriek in a nanosecond. 'Now, follow me to class.'

'I'm staying here and re writing this.' I picked up the torn paper and returned to my desk. Mrs Barton hesitated and then decided not to continue the argument. I remember shaking with anger and then fear, I'd heard people being expelled for less, could snatching those papers be counted as physical assault? I doubted it, anyway if she wasn't going to kick out Dean then I wouldn't be expelled, would I? I was too upset with all these thoughts to restart my essay and when Adam and Joe found me after class they thought we should go to the chippy for lunch so I could calm down.

Henry (Admin1)

Thursday, 29 March, 16:11.

A Star

I'm about to leave the IT room for my detention but I thought I'd write this up first. We were doing a mock exam in general studies and our teacher was very stressed about it. Mr Roth slipped into the classroom and crept towards my desk. Our teacher pretended to ignore him.

'A star for your coursework,' he whispered.

I grinned back at him and he attempted to creep out of the room but tripped over a bag strap and staggered into the whiteboard. He literally headbutted the board, knocking pens everywhere. The class started laughing, even our teacher chuckled. Mr Roth performed a mock bowed and left the classroom. We still had to work in silence for the rest of the lesson but everything felt was more relaxed.

Henry (Admin1)

Thursday, 29 March, 20:09.

Detention

Despite going to Norcrest Academy for seven years I have never received a detention. I've been in class detentions but those weren't my fault, it's where everyone has a detention despite the fact only a few kids were misbehaving. Technically I still haven't been in detention. I'm going to a mandatory revision class. Mrs Barton's revision class was in her history classroom.

'Sit down,' Mrs Barton said when I entered. 'You can do the work you missed in lesson yesterday.'

I took a seat, flicked open my history textbook and started answering the essay question. Mrs Barton continued to type at her computer.

I couldn't focus on my Mussolini essay. I don't care what happened in another country one hundred years ago. I care about what was happening now. Yasmin's abortion, my A levels, Mum and Dad. The essay was a waste of time. Almost everything we learn in school isn't relevant. Adam had raised this point on the school council last year but no one listens to us because we're only students. I'd only finished my introduction paragraph when someone knocked on the door.

Yasmin stood in the doorway.

'What are you in here for?' Mrs Barton sniffed without looking up from her screen.

'Bad attendance and talking back to a teacher,' Yasmin smiled.

'Bad attendance. That's putting it mildly isn't it? I don't think I can remember the last time I saw you in school. Which teacher were you rude too?'

'Mr Warren.'

'What did you say to him?'

'That he smelled like vinegar.'

'And why did you say something as stupid as that, Yasmin?'

'Because it's true.'

I masked my laugh as a cough.

'Sit down,' Mrs Barton ordered.

Yasmin strolled into the classroom. When she saw me she arched her eyebrows but said nothing. Mrs Barton's typing speed had decreased as though she was waiting for one of us to speak so I didn't attempt to.

We worked in silence for ten minutes until there was another knock on the door. Mr Sandil walked in.

'Are you coming to the Prefect meeting?' he said to Mrs Barton.

She swore. 'I forgot, I was too distracted babysitting these two. Tell everyone, I'll be there in five minutes.' She turned to me, 'I expect that essay to be finished by tomorrow morning.'

She snatched up her handbag and half ran from the room.

Yasmin flicked her the finger. 'What the hell are in here for?' she asked me.

I turned in my chair. 'I had a row with Mrs Barton.'

'Yeah?'

'I was meant to be in her class but I was doing homework instead.'

'Hardcore,' Yasmin rolled her eyes.

'She said, do you want to waste your life away by failing your a Levels and I said, what like you?'

It didn't sound as cool as I wanted it to but Yasmin's lips did flicker into a smile.

'That bitch in Dean's selfie is some prat called Elle. She goes to an art college somewhere. Dean's not been answering my calls or texts.'

'You shouldn't be calling him,' I muttered but Yasmin was already packing her bag. It explains why Dean hadn't jumped me outside the school, he was too busy with his new girlfriend. I threw my textbook, notepad and pens into my bag.

'How's it going with...?' I nodded to her belly.

'Not here, idiot,' she hissed.

'Sorry, I –.'

'She gonna email you?' Yasmin asked nodding to Mrs Barton's computer.

'Email me?'

'Yeah, whenever I used to get detentions she would email my Dad. I'd delete them first.'

I had no idea if Mrs Barton would email my mum or not but I was glad we'd already had parent's evening. Mum was already stressed from her new job and had been badgering me every night about my homework.

Yasmin walked to Mrs Barton's desk and shook the mouse. The screen flared into life.

I joined her and saw a dialogue box was open on the screen.

Username:

Password:

Yasmin typed in BBarton01 for the username and then hesitated.

'Dunno, the password. Hang on.'

'If she walks in,' I warned.

'Nah, she won't. Those meetings last ages.'

I looked at the door as though Mrs Barton was about to return. In reality she was likely going to be sitting in the Common Room with Adam and the other prefects discussing meaningless awards.

Yasmin typed something only for the computer to reject it.

'You thinking about going prom?' I asked.

'Dunno. Not thought about it. I doubt it.' The computer rejected another password.

'It'll be the last time we see anyone from our year.'

'Good. Ah.' The dialogue box on the computer was replaced by a loading symbol. 'Scott.'

'What? Was that her password? Is that her husband?'

'Nah, Who'd want to marry her? It's the name of her dog. I can't delete the email because she hasn't sent it yet. You'll have to do it when you get home. I can't actually do a lot,' she laughed, 'I can enter the homework list for your class, make a few changes if ya like.'

Yasmin returned to the desktop and she clicked on a document. Our homework checklist appeared on the screen.

'What homework haven't you done?' Yasmin asked.

I'd stopped writing about my essays on here because it depressed me. 'Those ones, there.'

I pointed out the unticked boxes. Yasmin filled them in with a few presses of the keyboard.

'Done,' she grinned. 'I'm gonna change her password.'

'Shit. Why?'

'Because she's a bitch and she deserves it. What were you saying about Prom?'

'There'll be a free bar.'

'Who else is going?'

'Everyone I think.'

A new dialogue box had opened on the screen.

Would you like to change your password? Yes/No?

Yasmin clicked Yes prompting another box to open.

Enter old password:

Enter new password:

Confirm new password:

'What should we change it too?' Yasmin asked.

'She'll know it was us, won't she?'

'Nah. She leaves herself logged in all the time. It could have been happened anywhere.'

Yasmin filled all three fields and pressed confirm.

'What did you type?'

'Her new password is Yasminissexyaf because it's true. C'mon.'

Yasmin marched out of the room, I followed her down the corridor.

'When can I... come over next to do some more research?' I asked.

'I dunno yet. I've got lots of revision to do.'

I was going to ask if she really thought revision was that important but we saw Megan and Chelsea waiting at the other end of the corridor. 'Shit, I gotta go. I'll speak to you later, yeah?'

Without waiting for an answer Yasmin ran towards her friends.

Mrs Barton sent an email to Mum that evening. I wonder how long it took her to get back into her account. I told Mum that I had gone to a revision lesson after school and when Mum fell asleep that evening I logged into her email account from my laptop. An email from Mrs Barton sat at the top of Mum's inbox, unopened.

Delete.

Henry (Admin1)

Friday, 30 March, 10:24.

Career meeting with Mrs Saunders

Adam was late to tutor today. He arrived as Mr Sandil was in the middle of his announcements.

'For those of you who want to go to university, Mrs Barton has kindly organised a summer school program between the sixteenth and twentieth of July,' Mr Sandil said. 'Lecturers and students will be coming to speak to you about University life. I recommend you all go even if you don't plan to go to uni. It'll teach you life skills.'

I might go to Summer School if only to hang with Adam and Joe if they choose to go.

Mr Sandil motioned for Adam to take his seat.

'Bunking tutor?' Jo asked him.

'I was putting these prom posters.' Adam pulled a poster out of his bag and slid it across to us. It looked like whoever had designed the poster had created it in a rush. Two figurers danced behind the words Leaver's Prom and the date Saturday 16th June.

'A Saturday?' I asked.

'Yeah, it was only time the hotel was free. If we booked it earlier than we would have gotten a Friday night.'

'I ain't wasting my Saturday at Prom,' Joe said.

Joe is the only person I know who isn't going prom. Yasmin had been tagged in Chelsea's Facebook status about Prom so I assumed she'd bought herself a ticket.

Joe snatched the poster back and started drawing on it.

'Boys,' Mr Sandil snapped.

I looked up, the class was staring at us.

'Sorry,' I muttered.

Joe, unabashed, passed the poster back to me. He'd labeled the dancers Henry and Yasmin. 'See, it'll be you dancing at your wedding.'

I swore at him as Mr Sandil turned back towards the board.

'There has been a change of plan with the year group photos. It will be taking place next week Tuesday, weather depending.' Mr Sandil announced this morning.

I didn't really care about the year group photo but I knew Mum would want one.

Grace raised her hand. 'I'm not going to be in. I'm on holiday next week.'

'Holiday during term time?' Mr Sandil asked.

'Yeah my Dad booked it.'

'You need to tell Mrs Barton.'

Mr Sandil then told us that everyone in our year was meant to have a fifteen minute meeting with Mrs Saunders about our career aspects in the future. I thought this was odd as Mrs Saunders hadn't talked about jobs to me in any of our previous sessions.

'I'm glad you coming to prom Henry,' Mr Sandil said when I approached him at the end of the period to buy my prom ticket. 'Did I see you in detention the other day?'

'Yeah.'

'For what?'

'Not doing homework. I've got other subjects to revise for.'

Mr Sandil frowned at me but his class arrived and he didn't have time to ask me anything else.

'You going to make Yasmin your prom Queen, then?' Joe asked in English as Mrs Hughes returned our Romeo and Juliet essays.

'Leave it, man.'

'Are you two seriously dating yet?'

'I thought she was with Dean?' Adam said.

I ignored them and looked at my rewritten *Romeo and Juliet* essay, it had been awarded a C.

'Aw, is that meant you be you?' Joe asked, circling the names Romeo and Juliet. I kicked him under the table.

'Henry,' Mrs Hughes snapped.

I froze.

'You need to see Mrs Saunders for your career meeting,' Mrs Hughes said putting down her phone. She hadn't seen my kick. As I packed my bag I tried to ignore Joe's kissing sounds.

When I opened her office door Mrs Saunders was slumped in her chair, her desk littered with empty coffee cups.

'Oh, hello Henry,' she said.

'You okay, Miss?'

'Oh yes, fine, fine. Just a caffeine shortage. I've been talking to everyone in your year. What job do you want in the future?'

I closed her office door and took a seat. 'Ideally? I suppose I could be a teacher. But like, not teaching. What you do.'

'An advisor?'

'Yeah, an advisor. Like that.'

'I think you might be good at that. You have enough experience. You'll need to take psychology at University.'

'I don't do psychology A level.'

'You don't?'

I was annoyed she couldn't remember what lessons I took. Maybe it was because she was tired. 'I take English lit, history, general studies and geography.'

'Oh. Okay, what about when you leave Sixth form? What do you want to do then?'

'Maybe go to college or University,' I answered, 'but I'm still looking into it.'

'You're leaving it rather late, Henry. You've only got till, what, April twentieth?'

'It's a really big decision,' I said quoting something Mum had said, 'so I want to look at all my options.'

Mrs Saunders didn't look impressed. 'And what about a Saturday job?'

'I don't think I should look for one now, being so close to the exams.'

'Everyone in your year group should be looking at getting jobs, even if it's close to your exams. Where do you see yourself working in the future? Maybe a shop on the high street like Primark or Marks and Spencer's? Would you like to work there?'

'No. I wouldn't want to be dealing with people.'

Mrs Saunders paused. 'Do you plan to find a job once your exams have finished?' she asked me.

'Yeah,' I lied. I'd heard stories of university students in their third years without jobs. I didn't know how they could afford a house or food but it must be possible.

'I'm sorry, I don't have much time today Henry, we'll book in another session next week. Before you go, is there anything you want to discuss with me?'

'No I'm good.'

'Are you sure? You can talk to me about anything, you know?'

I thought about telling her about Yasmin's pregnancy but I couldn't. There's so much going on, I couldn't marshal my thoughts. If I decided to tell Mrs Saunders everything, I wanted to know what I was going to say and not prattle on like an idiot.

'Yeah, I'm fine.'

Grace had a row with Mrs Barton about her holiday. Grace's dad has another business trip to Shanghai. It's only for a week and a half but Joe overheard Mrs Barton going mental. She threatened to take Grace off the end of year school trip to Thorpe Park but Grace said she didn't care. No one does to be honest. Grace left Mrs Barton's office crying apparently but she's going on holiday anyway which means she'll miss photo day.

Henry (Admin1)

Saturday, 31 March, 19:23.

Interview feedback

'I know why they did it,' Mum said when I came home from bowling with Dad. We'd had to leave the bowling alley early because Linda had texted Dad that her bathroom was leaking.

'Who?' I asked. She was watching *Death in Paradise* so I thought she had solved the murder before the detectives or something. Then I thought she had somehow discovered Mrs Barton's deleted email.

'Why Aglet didn't hire you,' she said, 'I was in their shop this morning. Do you remember when my sandal broke? I went to buy a new one today.'

Mum had mentioned something about her sandal breaking but I hadn't really been listening. I'd completely forgotten about my interview as well, to be honest.

'Everyone in there is either a really pretty girl or gay,' Mum stated.

I hadn't been in Aglet's shop so I just nodded. Mum spoke for a bit about how unfair it was but the real reason is that I suck at interviews.

Henry (Admin1)

Monday, 2 April, 21:30.

What do I do once school finishes?

Mr Sandil warned us that if we haven't applied for college or uni then we need to soon or all the places will be filled. When he told us Mrs Barton was still writing our references I freaked and actually wondered what Mrs Barton would say in mine after my detention with her.

Would she give me a shit reference because I pissed her off? She shouldn't do, professionally, but I wouldn't put it past her. I couldn't stop thinking about it and when I heard her shouting in the corridor for Will to lengthen his tie I literally jumped.

In general studies Bethany Holder announced, 'Oh my god, we've only got two weeks of Sixth form left.'

This triggered my anxiety. When the lesson was over I went to Mrs Saunders' office. She explained that everyone at school is feeling the same way about finishing Sixth form but that they're a lot better at hiding it.

We brainstormed my choices for after Sixth form.

University. The problem I have with this is that I don't want to move out. I could go to a university in London but there are none near me that offer a course I'm interested in.

College. There are lots of colleges in my area so I wouldn't have to move out. I still have the same problem as I do University, I don't know what I want to study. I'm scared of sacrificing three or four years of my life to something I won't enjoy.

Get a Job. I think this is the most feasible option. Mum says I shouldn't expect to get a really good job straight away but she says I could try and get a job in a shop. I would hate to work with the public but it is better than my final option.

Do nothing. Stay at home and play games all day. As much as I like that idea I know Mum won't allow it. She keeps saying that when she was my age she started an apprenticeship in hairdressing and when Dad left school he started a job the next week. The world is different now and I don't care what Mum and Dad were doing years before I was born. It isn't relevant to me.

I keep thinking about the girl I saw crying at Stanlow University. I don't want to become like her.

I applied for an English course at college this evening. Mum was ecstatic that I had made a decision and she helped me fill out the application form. Then she made a Facebook status about how proud she is of me. I felt fucking terrible, like I was a fraud but it got even worse when Dad asked me about it this evening. He asked me if that was what I really wanted to do with my life. I said yes. He asked me if I was sure and I said yes again. I could tell he didn't believe me though but I didn't know what else to say.

I've heard lots of people drop out of college within the first couple of weeks. Maybe I can do that and reevaluate what to do? Term starts in September.

Henry (Admin1)

Tuesday, 3 April, 14:38.

Year Group Photo

We met in our tutor rooms, marched out to the field and found that the photographer and his assistants had set up a series of metal steps. We lined up in tutor group order and then height order. I'm one of the tallest in the year so I was placed at the top of the steps and watched as everyone else took their place. Adam was forced to sit on a plastic chair in the front row with the prefects, teachers and Mrs Barton.

This picture is meant to show us united, be a memento for our parents and for us to look back on in future years. Of course, this photo doesn't represent the whole year group.

People are missing. Grace is on holiday in Shanghai, Yasmin is god knows where and several other people are sick or bunking off.

By the time the bell for period one sounded only half of the year group were in the correct places. It took another ten minutes for Mrs Barton to organize us and order Dean to stop mucking about. We smiled for the camera and suffered reshoot as raised fingers and bunny ears were displayed.

Throughout the day we were called out of our classes to have our individual sixth form photos taken in the Common Room. I didn't mind missing ten minutes of history. I sat on a cushioned seat in front of a screen, made sure my tie was straight and that the top button of my shirt was done up and smiled at the camera. My picture looked okay, Mum will be happy.

Henry (Admin1)

Tuesday, 3 April, 15:44.

Mum's Job

Doctor West asked how Mum was getting on at work today and I feel I should write about that. She says that the people there are nice but it's noisy. The ladies behind the counter gossip all day and listen to the radio. Mum insists that this is only a stepping stone until something better comes along.

Henry (Admin1)

Wednesday, 4 April, 10:32.

Year book quotes

This year our school is doing a yearbook for everyone leaving. They take our individual photos from yesterday, shrink them down and sell them in a book. Everyone is allowed to submit one personal quote in the school yearbook which was due at tutor time this morning.

Me: If you can't blow them away with your brilliance, baffle them with your bullshit.

Adam: Future Prime Minister in the making.

Joe: Maths is the second hardest thing in the morning.

Yasmin posted her quote on Facebook.

Yasmin: I cheated on all of my exams.

Henry (Admin1)

Thursday, 5 April, 21:07.

Parallel Parking

I'm okay at parallel parking but I don't see the point of it. After the fifth go I asked Colin, 'how often will I need to use this?'

'I use it everyday.'

His answer reminded me of when a student asks a teacher why they need to know something like Pythagoras' Theorem and they say, for your exams.

When I saw Dad this evening I asked him how often he parallel parks.

'Hardly ever,' he said, 'I always find a different parking space.'

Henry (Admin1)

Friday, 6 April, 23:59.

Adam's Play

I've been so caught up in my own problems, Yasmin, my exams, Dad, that I forgot about Adam's play. Adam takes drama and part of his coursework is to produce an adaptation of a film into a play and then perform it to a live audience. Adam was telling me and Joe in English that the plot is shit but they're marked on their acting. We agreed to go and support Adam but Joe said he was going to watch Bethany Holder's sister in the audience.

I nipped to the chippy with Joe that evening and we ate our dinner in the IT room.

'Where do you think we'll be after Uni or college or whatever?' Joe asked as he munched on his chips.

'No idea.'

'Do you think we'll have families and that?'

'I guess.' I knew that Mum and Dad had different boyfriends and girlfriends before they married each other. I couldn't see Joe as a Dad but maybe he would mature and grow into it.

'How many babies are you and Yasmin gonna have?'

'Fuck off man, that isn't even funny.' I slapped a chip out of Joe's hand.

'You gonna name your first son after me, right?' Joe laughed, 'Joe Andrews? I like that name.'

I ignored him.

'My sister's getting married,' Joe said after a while, 'to some builder bloke.'

'Yeah? Is he decent?'

'Yeah, he's alright. She's only twenty three though, just left Uni.'

I didn't see what the rush wash to get married. I knew a girl who left school last year ago and is already married.

'Maybe you can marry Yasmin?' Joe scoffed and I threw a chip at him.

We sat there awhile, I think Joe was wondering about the future, now that the end of term is so close everyone is panicking about it. I was thinking about my future. What would I do at university or college? What would I do after that? Would I move out by then? Would I be living in a bachelor pad or would I have a family? What I hate about the future is how uncertain everything is.

When Joe and I reached the drama building we found they were playing seventies music and a disco ball had been placed above the stage. We could see the curtain ruffling as the cast got ready. Then the drama teacher emerged from the curtain, said the play was about to start and everyone fell silent.

I didn't understand the play and I don't think Joe did either. Adam's acting was great though, his character was stabbed at a disco and Adam performed a monologue as he died. I hope Adam gets his A star. He deserves it.

Henry (Admin1)

Monday, 9 April, 22:01.

Final driving lesson

I had my final lesson with Colin today. Mum and I thought it would be best to stop lessons for now and pick them up again after my exams.

'Lots of students do it,' Colin said when I explained my decision to him. He then wished me the best of luck and told me to call him when I wanted to continue.

We've also decided to delay on doing my theory test. I haven't done any revision for it. Mum says she passed her theory test on her first try and her practical on her third. Dad told me it took him two attempts to pass both tests. I remember Dean boasting at school once that he passed on his first try but I doubt that's true.

Henry (Admin1)

Wednesday, 11 April, 19:44.

Moral Support

Yasmin texted me saying she wanted me to meet her at her house during my free double period.

'Where the fuck you been?' Yasmin said as she opened the front door.

Without waiting for an answer she led me into the front room and said she had something important to tell me. A voice in my head begged her to say:

I've told Dad about my abortion.

Or

I've decided to keep the baby.

or even

I've decided to phone a helpline and I've told an adult everything.

Yasmin said none of those things. 'I've booked myself in for the abortion.'

Her appointment was Sunday 29th April just before our exams. Yasmin said that was the only time the clinic had available and she couldn't wait any longer.

The clinic also said she should bring someone with her. She asked if I could go.

I promised that I would.

Henry (Admin1)

Saturday, 14 April, 15:21.

My Prom Suit

Mum insisted that I buy a new suit for the prom. We wandered around the suit department of Marks and Spencer's for forty five minutes before deciding on the second suit we had seen when we'd arrived.

'Prom is the most important school event, apart from your exams, of course.' Mum said on the drive home. She then told me how she was made Prom Queen when she left her school. Our school doesn't do Prom King or Queen but I let Mum talk about it and asked her questions like where she went to school and who were old friends were. She looked happier than I've seen her in a while.

Henry (Admin1)

Monday, 16 April, 17:34.

Revision

I've spent my free period going through all my textbooks and highlighting anything important. I've made flash cards and practiced a revision technique Mrs Saunders taught me. You think of a piece of information and you put that information in an area you know well, like your house. Then, in your mind, you travel from room to room and remember the information.

I'm most worried about my history exam because I have more information to remember. I need to know dates, people, locations, events, different records and then say which records are reliable and which ones are biased. In my English exam I'm going to be given a piece of text and using it with the other books I've read from my wider reading, I need to form an argument to a question. There isn't a right or wrong answer in English, it's all about how you support the point you make. That's fine if you believe what you're arguing but half the time I'm writing my answer because I have write something.

I'm confident in geography and general studies, the sooner I finish those exams the sooner I can focus on history and English.

Henry (Admin1)

Monday, 16 April, 18:04.

Break

Mum once said my body is like a car, it needs fuel/food to work. I think that the metaphor of my brain being a computer is better because it feels like I have too many tabs open. I've just read three pages of my history notes and didn't take in a word.

Henry (Admin1)

Monday, 16 April, 20:54.

Distractions

I've just come off the phone with Dad. He asked me how my revision was going. I said I kept getting distracted and losing my train of thought. Dad said I should block everything else out, stop procrastinating and focus.

That's easy for him to say.

Henry (Admin1)

Friday, 20 April, 21:26.

Last day of school

If Mrs Barton was expecting us to treat our final assembly as though it was going to be a lifelong memory, she was wrong. She had to shout for silence four times before she could start her speech.

'I know many of you have been looking forward to this day and what comes afterward for a long time. It's finally here. You're about to enter the big wide world. I know that some of you are excited, some of you are scared and some of you couldn't care less. We've tried our best to prepare you for what comes next. Hopefully you've learnt those lessons but there are some things that we can't prepare you for, things no one can prepare you for and for those times I wish you the best of luck. Those who try hard, those who do their best will always get what they deserve. I firmly believe in karma. And that's it. In six hours you're free.'

I wasn't listening but everyone clapped at the end. Then the school band brought their equipment before us. The school doesn't have an official band but Mrs Barton lets Will and his friends who study music play for us on special occasions. Will is the lead singer but when the song started the other band members played their instruments so loudly that you couldn't hear him. They're really shit but we clapped at the end anyway.

My first two lessons that day were general studies. We sat in the classroom chatting for two hours while a documentary played in the background. I kept browsing through the Mistveil Clinic's website on my phone. Every other review was positive. After break I had double English. Mrs Hughes had us watch that Romero and Juliet adaptation set in modern day America. The one with guns instead of swords, it was alright.

At lunchtime Adam, Joe and I headed to the IT room. They were talking about the trip to Thorpe Park, Joe claimed he was going to buy a VIP pass to skip the queues and Adam said Mrs Barton wouldn't let him. We were passing the reception area when Yasmin, Chelsea and Megan emerged. Judging by the smell I guessed they had been smoking in Jake's car.

'Hi,' I smiled to Yasmin. I saw Joe nudge Adam and wink.

'Hey,' Yasmin muttered.

Adam, Joe and I kept walking and Yasmin and her friends went in the opposite direction. I didn't mean to say hi to her, it was just automatic. I could hear Chelsea and Megan quizzing Yasmin about me.

Joe turned on the spot, put his fingers to his lips and wolf whistled.

Yasmin blushed.

'Not you, bimbo. You're Henry's snatch. That was for Meg. You love me Meg, don't you?'

Yasmin and Megan scuttled down the corridor, Chelsea followed them, shouting insults at us.

'What the fuck is wrong with you?' I asked when they were out of earshot.

'What? Nah, Hen. Don't tell me you don't actually fancy her, do you? Ah, Jesus, Hen.'

'What?'

'Are you blind? What the fuck you thinking about someone like her, for?'

I ignored him and passed through the reception door.

'Hen, maybe you didn't notice, mate, but our exams are next week. Now is not the time, I mean Jesus, now is not the time to fuck everything up. Especially for her.' Joe followed me into reception.

'And what's wrong with her?' I asked.

'C'mon, it's Yasmin Rivers,' Joe said as though speaking to a five-year-old. 'She's…'

'What?'

'I'm just saying you could do a lot better.'

The receptionist was telling us to quieten down. Adam stepped between me and Joe.

'Fuck off,' I said, 'you're pissed 'cause you wished it was you.'

'Yasmin's a slag,' Joe laughed but there was malice in his voice. 'She'll do it with anyone. Listen. You can get your dick wet at uni, alright, but your exams are literally days away.'

I wanted to see Joe bleed. I wanted to punch the sneer from his lips. The receptionist was shouting now but she was just background noise to me.

'If you were in my position you'd do the same thing. How often have you banged on about getting a girlfriend?'

'She isn't even fit for fuck's sake. Have you seen how fat she's got?'

Adam was saying something, desperate to defuse the situation. He was still between myself and Joe. I laughed at Joe's face. Joe blinked and then swung his arms at me like a demented gorilla. I back stepped and Adam caught Joe in a bear hug, shunting him back towards the corridor.

'If you're going to fuck her, fuck her. Be a man and do it before the year is up,' Joe screeched.

The receptionist was shouting into her walkie-talkie for teachers to come to reception. I didn't know what else to do so I ran out of the school and towards the street.

I was so pissed off that I walked to the high street and back to try and calm down but only made myself tired. Joe's always been a bit of a dick but he'd not been that out of order before. He's been lusting after most of the girls at school for ages and he's jealous he thinks I have a girlfriend. He's also super stress about his A levels, but so is everyone else.

When I entered Mrs Barton's class I took my usual seat by the window. Adam gave me a nod when he arrived but sat on the other side of the room. It was as though the school wanted to make its final hours over me as tortuous as possible. Mrs Barton had allowed us to watch a DVD but it was a World War One documentary. We were ten minutes into the film where I spotted twenty Sixth formers running between the buildings.

'What's happening?' Will asked standing up in his seat.

The crowd disappeared behind the science block, running towards the school field.

Will scooped up his bag and walked out of the classroom, unopposed. Mrs Barton, who had been sitting at the desk throughout all this, rolled her eyes but remained silent. Half the class followed him casting her anxious looks. When ten minutes had passed and Will hadn't returned everyone else began to drift out the room.

We found most of the year group on the field. There was seven a side football being played, the crowd roared as someone scored a goal. The field was lined by students sitting down and chilling, I spotted Jake playing A Flo Rida song at full volume on a portable radio near the fence with Megan and Chelsea. I don't know how Jake had got into the school, Megan probably helped him, if the teachers knew they would flip but it I couldn't be arsed to tell them. Some students were going around asking for autographs on their shirts or in books. I didn't have an autograph book, I thought we do that when we picked up our results and I didn't want to ruin my shirt, so I used my notepad.

It's strange how people who I had hardly spoken to said they would miss me.

I saw Adam and Joe sitting by the goalposts but I chose to sit with Grace by the school fence. 'Happy end of the school year, Henry.' Grace hugged me. 'I really don't want to go, you know?'

'Yeah.' Jake's radio was making my head throb.

'I mean I hate Norcrest, everyone does, don't they? But... I like the routine of it all. I wish I could stay longer.'

I didn't say anything. I didn't want school to end but I was also ready for it to finish. Does that make sense? I'll miss the people here and I'll miss the structure of the day but the teachers could fuck off. Grace and I watched the football match but when I crept away twenty minutes later no one noticed me leave.

Henry (Admin1)

Saturday, 28 April, 23:09.

Shit

Mum just told me that Dad wants to see me on the same day of Yasmin's operation. He wants to go to a pub and watch a football match.

Mum clearly picked up on my lack of enthusiasm because she said 'I think you should take a break from your revision, Henry.'

I couldn't say no. I've texted Yasmin telling her what happened. Here's what I wrote:

Me: Hey. I have to meet my dad in town before we go. I can't get out of it.

Yasmin: I'll wait for u outside Mistveil.

I don't know how long Yasmin will wait or how long the football match will last or if Dad will want to do something afterwards.

I'm screwed.

Henry (Admin1)

Sunday, 29 April, 02:44

The operation

Dad picked me up from my house at half nine. Unfortunately Uncle Patrick was visiting to watch the football with Mum and he started shouting at Dad through the front room window. As we left I could hear Uncle Patrick and Mum arguing over if Dad had the right to see me, which he completely does. He might be a bastard but he's still my dad. Dad drove us to the pub and spoke nonstop about the football match and how bad both side's managers were.

The football match hadn't started yet but everyone in the pub was watching the TV. It was even more crowded than the last time Dad and I were here. England flags had been hung above the bar and a group of lads by the snooker table were chanting a football song I couldn't understand.

We joined a table opposite the TV and watched the presenters for a few minutes. 'How's school, then?' Dad finally asked. I could hardly hear him over the noise.

'Fine.'

'You've got your A Levels coming up, haven't you?'

'Yeah. Next week.' I kept eyeing on the time on my phone.

'How you getting on with that girl?' Dad asked.

'What?'

'That girl you were seeing. Dark hair. The big one.'

'Yasmin, you mean?'

'Yeah. Yasmin. Lives opposite.'

'Yeah that's her. I'm meeting her afterwards actually.'

'Ah right. You seeing a film?'

'Yeah.' I stared at my phone and prayed Dad would shut up.

'What you gonna see?'

'Don't know yet. We'll have a look what's on.'

Twenty minutes later, the match started. Everyone in the pub watched the screen. I kept glancing down at my phone.

Yasmin: How long r you gonna b?

There was a loud cheer as someone scored a goal. The punter's roared. Dad clasped my shoulder.

'Did you see that? Ha. Hen, put that phone away.'

'It's important.'

'Put it away, you're missing the match.'

'No.'

The grip on my shoulder tightened. 'Hen, I've only got you for a small amount of time, alright? So act like-'

'Like what? That I want to be here?'

'Eh?'

'Whose fault is it that you have so little time for me?'

Dad just stared at me. I don't think he realised that I was arguing with him.

'You said you want to spend time with me,' I spat, 'but you spend half the time seeing Linda. If you're going to fuck off to Spain then hurry up and do it.'

'How'd you know about Spain?'

'Piss off.'

'Hen, I was going to tell you.'

I flipped him the finger.

Dad snorted, snatched his coat and stormed out of the pub.

I didn't stop to think about the repercussions, I ran for the bus stop.

Yasmin was waiting in the clinic's carpark, smoking. 'Where the fuck have you been?'

'With Dad. Just ditched him.'

Yasmin scoffed and lit another cig.

'Do you want me to go in with you?' I asked.

'No, I don't want you staring at my fanny. Just... stay here.'

Yasmin didn't go inside immediately. She paced back and forth in the carpark and burned through three cigarettes. She was about the light her fourth when she muttered 'fuck it,' pulled down her hood and marched into the clinic.

I watched her go, wishing she wouldn't leave me. I was scared, shitting a brick level scared but I knew I was doing the right thing by waiting. I'm not going to lie, I was also kind of pissed off Yasmin had asked me to come only to leave me outside. I didn't go into the waiting room though, in case they asked who I was.

I waited outside in this dumbed state of mind, too scared to do anything. An immeasurable amount of time later my phone vibrated. It was Mum and according to my phone this was her seventh call.

'Hello?'

'What happened with you and Dad? He's in a right-'

I hung up and turned off my phone.

When Yasmin emerged from the clinic, she looked pale but otherwise unhurt.

'It was fine,' she said after a moment, 'I had anesthetic. It didn't hurt too much.'

'Was it... okay?'

'I wouldn't say okay but yeah. It's done.'

I wanted to know more. I didn't want to know the details of the operation but I wanted to know... something.

'Well, what did they say?' I asked.

'They said they wished Dad was there but I told 'em that wasn't gonna to happen. They said if I'd kept it, it would have been a girl.'

Yasmin was quiet on the bus home and I didn't ask her anymore questions. She winced as the bus went over potholes but insisted she was alright. When we pulled up at her bus stop she said, 'goodbye Hen,' and hurried down the street. She was crying but trying not to show it.

Mum gave me a bollocking when I came home and demanded to know where I been. I said "out with Yasmin". Mum then made me phone Dad to apologise but he didn't answer my call.

She then explained that Dad told her about moving to Spain the day he'd come to pick up his stuff. Linda has a second house out there. Mum said I was invited to join them in the Summer but now she didn't know if I could go. I couldn't care less.

That night I saw Yasmin's bedroom light was on. I texted her.

Me: You ok?

The read receipt appeared on my phone but rather than a reply Yasmin turned off her light.

Henry (Admin1)

Thursday, 3 May, 19:01.

A level English Literature

I didn't hear from Yasmin in the morning but I was too stressed about my English exam to text her. My English exam was the first A level to be scheduled for my year group. My geography exam is the last. Before all of the A Levels and GCSE exams, the canteen serves us a free breakfast. It's a nice gesture but the food is shit. I took two pieces of toast and sat down at a table at the end of the hall. Joe and Adam joined me. Joe was too stressed with last minute revision to be angry at me. I was too nervous to argue. I scanned through *The Critical Reading Handbook of The Great Gatsby* as I nibbled on the toast. Mrs Hughes took a register and wished us luck.

'I still don't like Daisy,' Joe commented dropping a chunk of his toast on the floor.

I looked around the canteen. No sign of Yasmin. Dean wasn't there either but Megan and Chelsea were, laughing with their friends near the fire exit.

'You're not supposed to,' Adam said, 'I don't like Gatsby either, he loves Daisy but doesn't think about her daughter.'

I didn't add anything to their conversation, I couldn't stop thinking about Yasmin. She told me once that she would have taken English if it didn't clash with her Spanish class.

The bell for period one sounded and once the corridors had cleared we were herded towards the science block. We can't have our subject classrooms for our exams because the displays on the walls might give us the answers. We lined up outside the lab, put our bags at the front of the room and took a seat.

The invigilator was from the exam board, I hadn't seen her in the school before. She wrote up the start time and the end time on the whiteboard at the front of the classroom. We had two and a half hours exactly to complete the paper. A teaching assistant stepped among the desks replacing broken pens, answering any last minute questions and assuring us that we would do okay.

'You may begin,' the invigilator said and everyone turned over their exam papers.

I don't remember much about the exam except that I wrote six and a half pages and when it ended my hand was hurting from cramp.

'I did shit,' Adam said as we made our way to our IT room.

I didn't answer him.

'I rushed it,' he continued, 'I was too busy thinking about my maths exam later.' Joe and Adam bickered about the exam and compared their answers but I didn't want to talk about it until I picked up my results. We threw ourselves onto the swivel chairs in the IT room, settled down and then I reread my history revision.

Henry (Admin1)

Wednesday, 9 May, 20:36.

A level history

I didn't sleep well last night, I slept through the Cannon Street train passing. Wilfred didn't wake me up either, Mum did twenty minutes behind schedule. I got dressed, shoveled my breakfast into my mouth and reached the bus stop as the bus was pulling away. I had to wait half an hour for the next one which was packed with year seven's and eight's. When I went to my history exam I was completely out of it.

The exam started ten minutes late because we had year eleven's banging on the doors and jeering at us. When they were shepherded away by the teachers we were finally allowed to start.

You know that feeling you have when you have a fear building inside of you and you can't stop it and the fact you can't stop the fear makes the fear stronger? I had that feeling when I opened my test paper and saw the questions.

How far was Bismarck's control in Germany in the years 1878 to 1890 weakened by opposition in the Reichstag?

I had to read the question five times. I don't remember what I wrote as my answer but I know it was shit. When we were allowed to leave I ran straight out of school, brought a can of coke from the corner shop and sat on the school field so I could calm down.

I returned home an hour late. When Mum asked me where I had been I said I had been chatting to Adam.

'How did your exam go?'

'Hard.'

'Did you do your best?'

'Yeah,'

'Then what happens, happens.'

Henry (Admin1)

Tuesday, 15 May, 17:28.

AS Level general studies

My next exam, general studies, was almost a week later. When I reached the canteen Joe was already there.

'You alright?' I asked him.

'I fucked up my French exam.'

'Oh yeah?'

'I was talking to two other people in my class and they both gave different answers to the final question, the one worth thirty marks.'

'They might both be wrong,' I suggested.

'Nah, they're the smartest in the class, I'm fucked.'

There was an unspoken agreement between us not to discuss Yasmin. I could still sense Joe's disapproval though.

The general studies exam was exactly as we practiced in class and I finished half an hour before the end. I reread my answer, adjusted my handwriting and checked my spelling.

Will was sitting in front of me and had his head laid on his desk. I thought he was bored because most of the class had finished by this point but then I saw the girl next to him laughing. I couldn't see what was so funny. Then Will snored. Most of the class heard it. I looked at the invigilator but she was still reading her magazine at the front of the room. Someone hissed Will's name. A thrown pencil bounced off his chair.

'Quiet please, everyone.'

'Miss,' Bethany Holder raised her hand. A teaching assistant came over. We all watched as Bethany whispered into the assistant's ear who then turned around and prodded Will on the shoulder.

Will jerked awake, with a snort. Everyone laughed but when the invigilator collected our papers I saw Will had finished his exam so I didn't feel sorry for him.

Henry (Admin1)

Monday, 21 May, 23:52.

A level Geography

The invigilator, the same one from my English exam, had just sat us down when Yasmin sprinted into the room, followed by the teaching assistant. Yasmin mumbled an apology to the invigilator, flashed me a smile and took her seat on the opposite side of the room. Dean sniggered from the back row.

'Best of luck everyone,' the invigilator said, 'your time starts now.'

I turned over the paper and started jotting down my essay plan. I had only finished my first line when there was a boom from the back of the classroom. Grace, sitting a few rows behind me, squealed and Yasmin jumped in her seat. The boom was followed by another and then a clap. It took me a moment to realise the sound was a recording. The opening of Queen's "We Will Rock You" blasted through the classroom.

Dean pulled his mobile phone out of his sock.

'Hello?' he said into it as the invigilator marched towards him. 'Who's this?'

'I'm disqualifying you from this exam,' she snapped and snatched his paper. Dean followed her down the aisle to the front of the classroom.

'Hold on, I'll call you back,' he said still smiling. 'You're what?'

'Get out.'

Then Dean burst into a rant that I'm sure will turn into a school legend. 'It doesn't fucking matter anyway does it? This isn't even a real subject. I've failed the coursework so what's the fucking point, eh? What's the fucking point?' He grabbed the table nearest the door and flipped it over. The invigilator retreated to the teacher's desk as Dean swung open the classroom door and then slammed it shut so hard that a poster fell off the wall.

Everyone stared at the door. The invigilator composed herself, 'Keep working please. We'll allow you all another two minutes at the end to make up for the time lost.' Then she told the teaching assistant to find Mrs Barton and ripped Dean's paper in two. I swear, it was the most satisfying sound I've ever heard. The teaching assistant returned a few minutes later with Mrs Barton and the three adults had a hushed conversation at the front of the room.

Two hours later, when we were collecting our bags Grace was explaining to me how difficult she found the paper.

'Oh my God, that was so hard. I mean, did you understand the second question? I didn't. I didn't understand it at all. I hope my coursework pulls my grade up.'

Yasmin was shouldering her bag by the door, searching the corridor.

'I'll be back in a minute, Grace,' I said. 'Yasmin, hey.'

We took several steps away from the classroom but everyone was too eager to leave to pay us any attention.

'How are you feeling?'

'Good,' she said, 'it's all finished now, y'know?'

'Did you know Dean was going to do that?'

'I knew he was going to do somethin' but I didn't know what. He was talkin' about getting us all in on it, me and the girls but when we said no cos we wanted to actually do our exams, he got all pissy. I think the flipping table thing was genuine. He was going on and on about how pissed off he was with all the exams. Are you going on to Thorpe Park tomorrow?'

'Yeah, you?'

'Nah, I wasn't invited. You should go though, you'll enjoy it.'

I wanted to say more. I wanted to tell Yasmin that everything would be alright now but I couldn't find the right words.

When I got home that night Mum took me to the Harvester to celebrate the end of my exams. She told me to phone Dad and tell him how my final exam went but he didn't pick up.

I feel bad about shouting at Dad in the pub but more annoyed that I couldn't explain to him why. Hopefully Yasmin will start telling people about her pregnancy, now it's over and there's nothing anyone can do about it.

'When's results day, Henry?' Mum asked as Uncle Patrick brought us desert.

'Second of August.'

'That's ages away. What are you going to do throughout the Summer?' I could tell she wanted me to say get a job but instead I said,

'Norcrest is doing this summer school program. It's meant to be for people going to Uni or college but everyone is going just to chat.'

Mum said it would be good for me to attend but as we were paying the bill she said, 'You should really spend most of your free time job hunting, shouldn't you?'

Henry (Admin1)

Friday, 8 June, 11:45.
Thorpe Park

I wasn't looking forward to Thorpe Park. I don't like roller coasters and I had a feeling that the other rides would be too childish for me. Mum said I should go to reward myself and it was better than sitting in my bedroom playing Xbox all day. When I arrived the only seat left was above the toilet, in front of the fire door. I'd just sat down when I heard shouting at the school gate.

Mrs Barton had her back to the coach door, arms folded across her chest, blocking Dean's way.

'Why can't I fucking go?' Dean bellowed.

'To start with there was your behavior in the geography exam.' Mrs Barton answered. 'You could tell by her voice that she was enjoying herself. 'Did you really expect you would be able to come?'

'I deserve it, I did all my fuckin' revision. Nah, man. Nah. This is fuckin' bullshit, mate.' Dean swaggered around the carpark and I was reminded of a gorilla pacing around a cage in a zoo.

'Don't swear at me Dean.'

Everyone on the coach was listening, Bethany Holder giggled. Dean flipped her his middle finger.

'I'll fuckin' follow you up the motorway,' he shouted. I spotted his quad bike parked by the school gates.

'I highly doubt it,' Mrs Barton sniffed. 'I think you should leave the school grounds now, Dean. I'll see you on results day, if you can be bothered to turn up.' She stepped onto the coach and the driver closed the door.

I felt someone climb over the back of my seat and land next to me. 'Jesus Christ. Yasmin what are you-'

'Shh.'

Yasmin turned to the students behind her and held a finger to her lips. They were silent at once.

Two of the deputy heads were trying to talk to Dean but he was swearing at Mrs Barton through the coach doors.

'Will he actually follow us?' I whispered to Yasmin as the coach pulled away. 'Are those bikes allowed on motorways?'

'It doesn't matter unless he knows how to hotwire his bike,' she held out set of keys. 'I was just... I was protecting the trip. I'll give them back afterwards,' Yasmin promised but I didn't care either way.

We had reached the motorway when I saw Mrs Barton walking up the aisle taking a register.

'Henry... and Yasmin.'

I had no words. I honestly believed for a second or two that she would tell the driver to turn the coach around and drop us off back at school.

'I don't like those shorts Yasmin,' Mrs Barton said after a pause, 'They're too... revealing.'

Yasmin had decided not to wear her hoodie, Mum told me that today was going to be the hottest day of the year, and instead was wearing a T shirt and shorts. The shorts revealed her most of her thighs and I had been trying not to look at them. 'I didn't want my trousers to get wet on the rides,' Yasmin answered. 'Y'know? Representing the school and all that.'

Mrs Barton nodded and continued her patrol of the coach.

'Christ, I thought she was gonna chuck you off,' I said.

'Dunno why she didn't,' Yasmin shrugged, 'anyway, I want to go on The Phantom.'

The Phantom was meant to be one of the fastest roller coasters in England. During the test runs the dummies fell out of their seats and the ride gained a reputation which only attracted more thrill seekers.

'You've got to go on it,' Yasmin said. 'It's like, the very reason I studied so hard at school this year.'

'You haven't got ninety three percent attendance,' I pointed out.

'Ok, it's the reason you studied so hard all year.'

When The Phantom was in sight I think a part of me died. Metal rails coiled above the tree line. A cart shot down the track and rolled a complete 360 degrees before disappearing from view. There was a gasp of delight from the coach.

'No,' I said.

'We've got to go on it.'

'No.'

'Don't be such a pussy.'

'No,' I said again but I felt like a pussy. When we got off the coach Mrs Barton gave a speech about where to go in the case of an alarm and a general talk not to be too stupid that everyone ignored. Then she handed out our tickets.

Everyone dashed for the turnstiles, clutching our tickets.

'Why'd Mrs Barton give you a ticket?' I asked Yasmin as we navigated our way through the barriers. I saw Mrs Barton was watching us from the coach, chatting to the driver.

'Dunno. She gave me hers. She said she hates going on rides. C'mon.' Yasmin snatched my hand we sprinted into the park, following the crowd towards the Phantom.

My excitement of being with Yasmin soon faded. I don't know what was worse. The anticipation of the ride or the ride itself.

After an eternity under the sun we reached the Phantom's loading platform. Yasmin wanted to sit in the front row. I wanted to sit literally anywhere else. We actually got the seats second from the front and when the protective barrier clamped down around us with a crash I squealed.

'Smile, dipshit,' Yasmin said but then she screamed as the cart jerked forward. You know how the cart is meant to go slowly up the first hill and then race around the rest of the track? Bullshit. The cart fucking flew up the first hill. I was completely unprepared.

'Put your hands in the air,' Yasmin shouted as we reached the summit.

My hands were wrapped around the safety barriers so tight my knuckles were white.

For a moment the park was laid out before us. You could see the children running around, fueled by the energy drinks being sold at ridiculous prices. You could see the other rides and hear the screams of their travelers mixed into a single roar. You could see the swarms of tourists in the car park milling around cars and coaches.

Then the rides shot down so fast I felt like I was a bullet being fired from a gun. I emitted a scream that was only broken by my need to draw breath so I could scream some more. At the bottom of the slope the track twisted to the left. Our cart turned onto its side, it felt like my stomach was trying to escape my body. The world before me was a blur, I couldn't distinguish between the sky and the ground. I closed my eyes but that made everything feel worse. The G force glued me into my seat as the cart spun on the corkscrew that was visible from the motorway. The wind was deafening I almost couldn't hear Yasmin screaming, not in the certainty we were going to die but in delight. She wasn't even holding onto the safety barrier.

That was stand out moment of my day, riding The Phantom with Yasmin. We spent the rest of the morning going on the tamer rides and the afternoon we spent in the shade of the arcade liberating teddy bears from their glass prisons. When we returned to the coach at five o'clock, everyone was hyper.

'Let's go back to mine afterward,' Yasmin said as the class jeered at passing drivers. 'Dad's got a meeting in London and his drink cupboard is full.'

I'd never been upstairs in Yasmin's room before. I'd only ever seen a snippet of her room from my window. Turns out that under the posters of models and boybands, her wallpaper was a dull pink. Clothes, empty bottles and dirty plates littered the floor. Yasmin had a desk at the end of her bed, similar to my own, only hers was stained with makeup. The room stank of perfume.

Yasmin's bed wasn't made and she was really embarrassed about it. She told me to sit on the floor, poured us two glasses of wine and joined me. She drained her glass instantly and refilled it from the bottle. Within twenty minutes she was giggling nonstop.

I don't remember what we talked about for most of the evening but it was relaxing to not talk about the operation or our exams. At one point Yasmin was talking about Dean.

'But seriously he was a complete cock,' she snorted.

I took a sip of wine to show my agreement. I didn't like the taste or how it made my head feel warm but I drank it anyway.

'He broke up with that other girl, by the way. Did you know?'

'No.'

'Well they broke up after two weeks. Serves that bitch right. She put it all over her

Facebook wall. What do you think? About Dean?'

'What'd you mean? Why's he such an arsehole?'

'Yeah,' Yasmin snorted, 'he can be nice though, sometimes.'

'Can he?'

Yasmin shrugged and leaned back, hitting her head against her desk. A piece of paper fluttered down. As Yasmin hiccupped I scooped up the paper. It was a copy of her CV. It was only half a page long. How could such an amazing girl could create such a small impact on the world?

Yasmin's head fell on my shoulder, her hair brushing my chest. I rested my head against her.

If this was a film we would have kissed and started making out.

But life isn't a movie. Nothing happened.

Yasmin dozed. I was disappointed but then I felt bad for feeling that way. Yasmin's got enough to worry about without me. I got bored and worked on my blog on my phone. When Yasmin woke up we watched YouTube videos of people on rollercoasters, drank some more wine and then I went home. I think I threw up on the railway bridge because Mum said when I came in at two in the morning there was sick on my shoes.

Henry (Admin1)

Saturday, 16 June 10:41.

The Prom

The prom wasn't too bad in the end. It was yesterday but I've only just got round to writing about it. In America, especially in films, they always make a big deal out of prom. The main character will always be asked or ask someone to prom where the movie will end as the hero and his or her lover slow dance. That doesn't happen in real life or at least in England but Doctor West said I should try and enjoy myself.

Mum took about twenty pictures of me in my new suit before dropping me off at the Vaughan Hotel. Mr Roth was wearing a tuxedo and talking to Grace who was wearing a cream dress and had done her hair up. Mrs Barton was talking to the barman and Bethany Holder was posing with her friends for a selfie. Adam said hello to me but then he spoke to the other prefects so I didn't feel like I could talk to him. There was no sign of Joe.

Yasmin arrived ten minutes later. She had chosen a pink dress with an open back. Her dress hid her legs, she sort of glided across the reception towards me. 'Hello,' she said.

'Hi. Nice dress.'

'Thanks, I feel like a Disney princess. It's so uncomfortable though.'

It had only taken me ten minutes to get ready for prom but I knew from Facebook that Bethany Holder and her friends had taken three hours doing each other's hair and makeup.

I wish I'd bought a better suit.

Yasmin ordered drinks. I joined Will and his friends as they watched a magician Mrs Barton had hired perform tricks. They laughed, as the man made Will's credit card disappear only to reappear in Will's inside pocket. Will then snorted his drink out of his nose and the magician made another drink appear from within his cloak.

Then I realised something. This was going to be the last time I'll see most of these people. Some are going to move away to start new lives at Uni, others will start full time jobs and others will just fade away. Do you know where your friends from primary school are? How many of their names can you remember? They used to be the most important people in your life and now they're nothing.

I've heard the expression your school years are the best years of your life and I hope that isn't true.

'Smile, it's a party,' Yasmin said as she returned with two full glasses.

She was right. I wanted to enjoy the time I have left with them. I also wanted my last memories of them to be drunken wrecks so I could feel better about myself later.

I sipped my drink and Yasmin updated me on a fight she had had with Megan and Chelsea that afternoon. Then Yasmin said she wanted to dance and after hiding her high heels under the table, we joined the throng of dancing students. Dancing is the wrong word. It was a mixture of grinding, awkwardly gyrating and in some cases just straight up dry humping. I had no idea what I was supposed to be doing but Yasmin seemed impressed.

I don't know how much time had passed when it happened. Somebody collided into me and I staggered into the DJ stand, landing flat on my arse. The glass I was holding shattered. The room cheered. Yasmin shouted, I could see her lips moving but the music stole her words.

'Dancewithme,' Dean's words were little more than one slur. He was clutching a half empty can of beer.

I tried to stand but the room was spinning and I couldn't hear what Yasmin or Dean were saying. It was like someone had muted a TV and I was watching actors mime their lines. Dean flung down his can which spat beer across Yasmin's dress.

In hindsight he probably wasn't going to hit her. I staggered towards Dean, grabbed him by his shirt collar and shoved him. It wasn't very aggressive or masculine or anything like that but it was enough to piss him off.

The DJ turned his microphone on just as Yasmin shouted, 'If you don't fuck off Dean I'll tell everyone about your chlamydia.' There was a pause and the room erupted into laughter. Mrs Barton stepped between us and Dean. I thought he was going to her, he was shaking with anger. Instead Dean opened his mouth and projectile vomited down Mrs Barton's dress. She screamed and Dean sprinted out of the room, his hand covering his mouth, vomit trickling through his fingers. The crowd cheered as the DJ turned the music back on, the hotel staff fetched mops and Yasmin made the tables our dance floor.

Henry (Admin1)

Saturday, 23 June, 10:57.

The Average

Yesterday, when I had finished eating dinner, I heard my phone ringing in my bedroom.

I had five missed calls from Yasmin.

'Where have you been?' she asked.

'Eating dinner.'

I'm not sure but I thought I heard her scoff before saying, 'I have two tickets to see The Average in London. Wanna come?'

'Yeah, sure.' I have no idea what she was talking about.

'We'll have to get here quick. The train is in ten minutes.'

'What?' but she had already disconnected.

I threw on a pair of jeans and a hoodie. Mum was laying on the settee, Wilfred asleep across her lap.

'I've got to go,' I told her picking up my house keys.

'Huh?'

'I'm going out. Yasmin just phoned me.'

'Oh, where?'

'A music gig, I think. It's in London.'

'Okay. Well… what time will you be back?'

'I don't know. I won't be late back, I promise.'

As I ran through the unmanned ticket barriers, the train's doors began to close. Yasmin was on the platform. She stuck her hand between the door's sensors and shouted 'c'mon.'

The few passengers onboard gave us bemused looks as I staggered onboard.

'Who're The Average?' I panted as we found two free seats.

'How… how can you ask me that?' Yasmin slapped the logo on the front of her hoodie. I recognised it as one of the logos from the poster of her bedroom wall.

'I thought you liked The Average, anyway?' Yasmin asked as our respective houses flickered into view.

I might have said that to impress her at some point. 'Play me some of their music.'

Yasmin pulled her phone out of her back pocket. 'Think of this as a spiritual awakening,' she said as she pressed played on their album. The first song was called "Cold Embrace." The main singer, Yasmin called him a "total babe" wasn't really pronouncing his words but Yasmin was singing along.

"I wish you were mine, I wish I was told, you were a criminal, the best in the world."

We finished the album before reaching London and when we emerged from the tube Yasmin was bouncing on the spot. We followed the crowds through the docklands, passing the closing shops and side stepping the con artists trying to sell us fake tickets.

'In there,' Yasmin pointed to a small warehouse next to the river. A crowd had already assembled inside and lights flashed out of the warehouse's door. I watched a group of girls exchanged their tickets for a plastic wristband with a security guard at the entrance. 'I've been here tons of times. It's fucking brill. Oh shit.' Yasmin clutched the side of her jeans.

'What?'

'The fucking tickets. They're at home. I left them on the fucking table.'

She howled and kicked a can of coke that was sitting in the kerb. 'I've waited for this gig for fucking ages. Look Hen, I'm so sorry I-'

'It's fine. It's not your fault. We can do something else, can't we? I think we passed a Weatherspoons on the way here. Or-'

Yasmin held up her hand. 'Nah, you give up too easily. I'm not about to walk away from this. I deserve to be in there. C'mon. We're improvising.'

I asked Yasmin why she couldn't load the tickets on her email but she said she didn't know her password.

We circled around the warehouse searching for another way in. 'I snuck in through that fire door last year,' Yasmin said pointing to the fire door at the back of the building. 'It leads you backstage.'

I pushed the handle of the door. Locked.

'Could you open it from the other side?'

'Yeah, if I get in.'

We returned to the entrance and watched the crowd inside. The first warm up band had started, the crowd was bathed in the colours projected by the lighting rig. Set up along the walls of the warehouse were stalls selling merchandise like CD's and posters.

'I've got an idea,' I said to Yasmin. 'I saw it on TV. We need to go back to the shops by the tube.'

We ran into a Ryman's that was about to shut and I brought a clipboard, a lanyard, A2 sized paper and marker pens.

Outside the shop I wrote down items I thought the stall owners would be selling. I hadn't been to many music gigs before so Yasmin helped me work out the prices.

T shirts: £10.00

Hoodies: £25.00

Limited Edition hoodies: £30.00

Album 1: £25.00

Poster 1: £10.00

Poster 2: £15.00

Poster 3: £10.00

We also wrote down deals in which you could buy two posters and get a third half price or win a limited edition hoodie if you entered a raffle. Outside the warehouse I gave the clipboard and list to Yasmin. She approached the security guard, while wearing the lanyard and I watched from a safe distance.

'Excuse me,' Yasmin said tapping the guard's shoulder.

'Yeah?' He towered over Yasmin, I could see the lights of the gig reflecting of his bald scalp.

'I need to get back to my boss' stand.'

'Can I see your pass?'

'I lost it.' Yasmin showed him her empty lanyard. 'I work for Stephen Newton,' She added helpfully. 'Do you know him?'

'No, hang on. 'ere, Don. You know a Steve Newton?' I heard him ask a second security guard, 'One of the stall owners?'

'Stephen,' Yasmin corrected. The main problem was that Yasmin was wearing her Average hoodie and I doubted the stall owners inside would be wearing their own merchandise. We'd turned it inside out and hid the hood as best we could. The Average logo was almost unnoticeable. I couldn't hear what the response was but both the guards looked uncertain.

'Do you want me to ring him?' Yasmin offered.

'Yeah, go on.'

Yasmin dialled a number into her phone. I answered her call.

'Hello?'

'Is that Mr er.... Newton was it?'

'Yeah, that's me. Can I help you?'

The guard paused. 'I've got a er… girl here for you. Says she works for you. You inside?'

'Yeah. She lost her card and can't get in?'

'Yeah.'

'She left it here, send her through.'

'Yeah, alright then.'

I watched as Yasmin was ushered inside then I sprinted to the back of the building. I didn't have a clue how long Yasmin would need to reach the fire door. I kept eyeing the time on my phone. After ten minutes, I heard the first warm up band finish and the second band start.

What if she leaves you here?

I ignored the voice in my head but I had a horrible image of Yasmin dancing away in the crowd without me. I checked my phone, dropped it back in my pocket and pulled it out when I could have sworn I felt it vibrate.

She's just using you, the voice said again.

I tried to distract myself. I looked across the river as a party boat passed by. Everyone onboard seemed to be enjoying themselves too. Behind the boat I could see an odd structure, something stumpy and grey. Then I realised it was the ruins of the Milton Mills Factory and I was at the warehouses I saw from my school trip. I could see the lights of the luxury flats twinkling in the empty sky down river.

They look over nothing but wasteland and warehouses. It isn't much of a view.

'Hey, Henry?'

Yasmin was leaning out of the fire door, her body illuminated by white light.

'You wanna come inside?' She smirked.

I swear I'd never seen someone so beautiful.

The fire door led us behind the stage, among the crew members. Wires coiled around our feet, the band were performing a few feet away from us, on stage but the way was blocked by security guards. A curtain separated us from the crowd.

Yasmin took my hand and we crawled under the curtain, avoiding the wires as though they were barbed. We emerged to face the first row, between us and them was a metal fence.

'How'd you get through?' A security guard shouted.

'Pushed.' Yasmin nodded at the fence. 'Let us back in?'

The guard held apart two panels of the metal fence and we slipped into the front row.

Result.

I've called it a music gig but I don't know if that's the right word. I'm not sure if it was a rave, or a festival, I think festivals are outside and last a couple of days but I do know that when The Average came onstage Yasmin and me danced through all their songs for two and a half hours. Yasmin screamed practically nonstop and at one point the lead singer looked right at us as he sang "Cold Embrace."

When we disembarked the night bus in the high street it was three in the morning. The muscles in my legs ached like they had done the morning after prom.

'That's was fucking fantastic,' Yasmin squealed.

'Yeah, that was brilliant.' In fact, I think it was the best night of my life. I do feel guilty typing that. I've so many good memories with my family but I do genuinely feel as if this was the best night of my life.

'I didn't know you liked The Average so much,' Yasmin said as she lit a cigarette.

'Yeah…' I watched as the end of the cigarette glowed orange and the ash fluttered to the pavement. Yasmin's eyes were wild, the cigarette pursed between her lips.

'Can I have one?' I asked.

'Have what?'

'A cig.'

'You… want to smoke?'

'Yeah, I wanna try one.'

It wasn't a nice smell exactly but at the same time it wasn't unpleasant either.

'Sure? Cause I don't want you to waste it. Have one drag then give it back.'

I took the cigarette and inhaled. I've never had a feeling like it, so it's hard to describe. It was sort of a giddy feeling in my head. That's a shitty description but it's the only way I can describe it.

Then I started choking.

'Don't be a smoker Henry,' Yasmin laughed, 'It's too expensive. You coming to my party next week?'

'Yeah. What's the party for?'

'Just because. I'll text you about it. I'm going this way home, see you later, yeah?'

Yasmin smiled again and leaned towards me. Her arms opened for a hug which turned into a squeeze.

But nothing more.

As we embraced I could smell a mixture of perfume and nicotine.

Henry (Admin1)

Saturday, 30 June, 21:37.

Henry

My name is Yasmin Rivers and Henry Andrews is dead. I'm so sorry.

Yasmin (Admin2)

Sunday, 1 July, 17:21.

Aftermath

I've known Henry since I was five years old when his family moved in opposite mine. In the last couple of months Henry has been nothing short of amazing. I can't tell you how sorry I am or how much I'll miss him.

Two days ago Henry OD'ed in my front room. This is what I remember.

I wanted a party at my house to celebrate the end of the school year. There wasn't much to celebrate, I'd missed most of school, had my abortion and probably failed my exams but I wanted a fucking party. I'd thought it'll cheer me up, you know? Dad was going to be away for a week hiking up the Scottish mountains with Clara so I'd have the house to myself.

I'd made a Facebook event and invited everyone I knew. Megan and Chelsea arrived at eight to help me set everything up. When Jake arrived at nine with his DJ kit I told him to set it up in the front room by the TV. I didn't like the idea of him DJ-ing because the neighbours might complain about the noise but I didn't feel like I could stop him. You can't stop Jake when he's made up his mind, he's a stubborn arsehole.

Dean arrived at half nine with five of his friends. We've been texting since his storm out in the geography exam and I'd said sorry for telling everyone at prom he had chlamydia. He's said he's sorry about sleeping with that other girl and said what a bitch she is. He can be nice when he wants to be but he can switch. I felt a bit guilty about stealing his bike keys but he didn't deserve to go to Thorpe Park.

Henry arrived just after ten. I didn't think he would actually come. He was wearing suit trousers and a T shirt with a collar, everyone else was wearing ripped jeans and stuff like that. You could tell he felt out of place, he was the only one who wasn't high or drunk. I was going to talk to him but I got distracted by one of Dean's friends puking up in the kitchen. Dean helped me clean it up and we watched one of his friends try to ride my bike around the garden but he was so high he couldn't stay on. Then Dean asked if he could have a quiet word with me upstairs so I took him to my room. I'd had a lot to drink at that point and I didn't care what we did. Dean can be a bastard but he's a fit bastard. As I went up the stairs I remember seeing Henry sitting near Jake's DJ kit typing on his phone.

The next thing I remember was Megan bursting into my bedroom screaming, 'He won't wake up, he won't wake up.'

'Who?' Sick rushed up my throat.

I knew who she meant before she said his name. 'H-H-Henry…'

I scrabbled out of bed and got dressed. Dean was shouting but I wasn't listening to what he was saying.

As I staggered downstairs two men wearing green and white jackets charged through the open front door. I saw the ambulance outside, its blue lights flashing through the doorway. Megan pointed into the front room and the two men ran through.

The house reeked of BO, nicotine, booze and weed. Everyone was standing around, as though in a trance.

Then someone shouted 'police' and everyone scattered. Two boys I didn't know collided into each other as they tried to escape through the front door. I remember Dean shoving past me, spotting the police car outside the front door and then legging it towards the back. I stayed at the bottom of the stairs, too stupid to move. Chelsea lead me outside but not before I saw the paramedics kneeling over a lifeless body half hidden behind Jake's DJ kit.

A policeman tried to ask me questions in the back of an ambulance but the paramedics insisted they look at me first. They did all these tests asking me to say stuff, shining a light in my eyes and asking me to open and close my fists. In the end they gave me a blanket and told me to sit still.

I watched more policemen arrive and go inside my house. I felt disconnected from what was happening as though I was in the back of a car and someone else was driving. The police were speaking to those who had remained or taking them to ambulances to be looked over. I don't know how long I sat there. Eventually the same policeman from before came back to talk to me.

'Excuse me, are you the home owner?'

'I... I live there, yeah.'

'What's your name?'

'Y...Yasmin. It's my.... It's my dad's house.'

'How old are you Yasmin?'

'Eighteen.'

'Yasmin, I need you to listen to me. Okay. I know you're going through a lot but I'll need you to answer some questions. Alright, can you manage that with me?'

'Is he dead?' I asked.

'At the moment we're-'

'Is he dead, though?'

The way the policeman looked at me, I swear. 'Somebody has passed away, yes. Do you think you can come back to the station to do a statement with me?'

'You're not under arrest at this point,' the policeman said in the interview room, 'we just want to find out what happened.'

I knew he would arrest me, if not now then later. I hadn't smoked anything last night but everyone else had and it was my house. He explained that he was going to record the interview and I agreed that he could. He brought in a woman to act as a responsible adult and to help me.

'This is Sergeant Rickman, the date today is Saturday 30th June 2018. State your name for the tape please.'

'Yasmin Rivers.'

Then he asked me tons of questions. 'Are you the home owner?'

'I live there.'

'Was it your party?'

'Yeah.'

'How many people were at the party?'

'Around fifty.'

'Did you know there were drugs there?'

'Yeah.'

I don't remember everything he asked. At one point I asked the responsible adult if I could go home. She explained that they were treating my house as a crime scene but I could stop the interview any time I liked. I asked if I could phone my Dad. Sergeant Rickman said they had already tried but I was more than welcome to try again. It went straight to voicemail.

'Is there anyone else we can call for you?' he asked.

'No.'

I agreed to continue the interview. Sergeant Rickman asked me for a list of people at the party. You know the house parties you get in shows like *Skins* and *Fresh Meat*? It was just like that, a proper rave. I didn't know everyone there, there were friends of friends but I assumed they were safe. I told Sergeant Rickman about the Facebook page but I knew more people had turned up. He promised he would contact them all. When we finished the interview, he gave me a card with the case number and his own number to ring just in case I remembered anything else. Then he offered to have someone drive me home.

Two policemen were waiting outside the front door when I arrived. Everything was the same from when I left. The fallen bottles and cigarette butts were still there. Jake's DJ stuff sat in the front room. There was a pile of people's coats on the kitchen floor. I looked at the spot where Henry's body has been. That patch of carpet looked darker than the rest but I don't know if I was just imagining that.

Yasmin (Admin2)

Sunday, 1 July, 19:17.

Dad phoned

Dad explained he'd just reached a hotel and he found the messages on his mobile from Sergeant Rickman. The soonest he could be back was tomorrow morning. He then told me to explain exactly what happened. I did and the phone call took two and a half hours. I've not remembered anything else. We don't know any adults in the local area to stay with me, we don't have any family living nearby but I promised Dad I would be okay.

Yasmin (Admin2)

Monday, 2 July, 03:23.

Henry's light

Last night, my phone wouldn't stop buzzing. Dean kept leaving me voicemails asking what the police had said. Megan and Chelsea were texting me. My Facebook notifications told me people were posting on my wall. I didn't have the energy to answer any of them.

I got out of bed at three to use the loo. My curtains weren't shut so I could see Henry's bedroom window. It was like I had been punched in the stomach. His mum had closed the curtains and his light was off. It seemed so final and definite. I ran to the bathroom to puke.

Yasmin (Admin2)

Monday, 2 July, 09:12.

How I found Henry's blog

You're probably wondering how I found Henry's blog. I was sitting in my room the morning after the party when I remembered that I saw Henry typing on a blogging website once, after Thorpe Park I think, and I remembered the title. I found Henry's blog on Google. I've read everything. The blog dates back to January, I don't know whose been viewing the blog but I've made myself an account. Although I can add to the blog, like you add comments to a Facebook status I can't use Henry's log in. I don't know his password.

There's an unpublished post saved under drafts but my account doesn't have access to it. I've tried to guess Henry's password.

Henry Andrews. Henry Andrews01. Wilfred. Wilfr5d.

No luck.

Here's the thing. I don't want to speak ill of the dead but Henry was a major arse. He's posted all of my details online. It might as well be a fucking Buzzfeed article,

When this eighteen year old got pregnant you'll never guess what she did next!

I've read all of Henry's posts, it's clear that he was obsessed with me. Lots of boys have been and will be obsessed with me but Henry thought that everything would be better if I loved him. I loved Henry but only as a friend, he was a literal NiceGuy.

Do you want to know why I told Henry about my pregnancy? He wasn't special, I hadn't really spoken to him since primary school. The truth is that I had to tell someone when I was standing at the Thames or I would have gone mad. Henry just happened to be there. I couldn't shake him afterwards so I let him hang around. I knew he wouldn't tell because that's the sort of boy he was but I didn't love him like a boyfriend. He kept seeing all these signs because he wanted to. Like when I smiled at him when we were looking up Universities with Mrs Barton. Megan had told me a joke, literally, the second before we walked into the room.

Henry needs to get his fucking priorities sorted, like when he was visiting Stanlow uni with Adam.

"I'd been thinking about what Yasmin would be like at University and what the other girls there would be like but I didn't know how to say this to Adam so we stopped talking about it."

There are more important things than having a girlfriend. I mean, Christ. I know I'm a hypocrite but I was never going to get the grades to go uni, anyway. Henry was something, y'know?

Yasmin (Admin2)

Monday, 2 July, 13:43

Dad's back

Dad came home today. I was on the settee trying to read *The Great Gatsby* because I knew Henry had read it and I wanted to keep myself busy. I'd wanted to take English in Sixth form but it clashed with my Spanish lessons. I don't think Henry did well in his English A Level, he didn't understand Gatsby. Gatsby isn't the good guy, he wants to ruin Daisy's life to make himself feel better. He wants to collect her and make her his trophy wife.

Anyway, when Dad arrived he wailed, 'Yasmin,' and wrapped me in his arms.

Dad cried because his train from Scotland had been delayed by a tree on the line and he couldn't get home any sooner. We had a deep conversation that I won't type out here but we both cried a lot. At the end of our talk Dad told me he had tried phoning Henry's mum but she wasn't answering her phone.

We deep cleaned the house and threw out what wasn't ours. Half drunk bottles of whiskey, coats that had been forgotten, Jake's DJ kit is gone. We burnt them in the garden, I couldn't look at them without seeing Henry's body. When we finished, I showered I felt a bit better.

Yasmin (Admin2)

Monday, 9 July, 22:59.

Formally Identified as Henry Andrews

Henry's death has made page three of our local newspaper. The first two pages were about a local flood but no one died. The newspaper is also published online and Henry's article has been shared around Facebook. Here's what it said:

"An eighteen year old boy who died of a suspected overdose at a house party has been formally identified as Henry Andrews. It was believed Henry was attending a friend's party when he died. Tributes and messages of condolences and grief have been pouring in on social media."

The article then gave quotes. I only recognised two of the names.

"Mrs Carol Andrews said 'My family is devastated by Henry's sudden death. There is a gaping hole in my life that cannot be filled.'"

'Henry was a brilliant person, you couldn't have met anyone better. I can't believe such a bad thing happened to such a nice person,' said Joe McNally, one of Henry's many friends.

There was also a statement from the school. "'We are shocked and saddened to hear of Henry's death. Henry had completed his A Levels and was looking forward to a bright future.'"

Joe's comment *pissed me off*. "One of Henry's many friends". Henry didn't have many friends, he had Joe, Adam, me and that's it. His comments about Henry being a nice person are stupid. When someone dies in a gang fight and it makes the news everyone goes on about how they were such a good person. Clearly they weren't. Henry was genuine.

Random people from school were posting things on Henry's Facebook wall.

"It was an honour to have known you."

"I'll miss you forever."

"You were a good man."

It made me want to punch something. They didn't know Henry, like I did. Henry said it himself.

"It's strange how people who I had hardly spoken to said they would miss me."

I left my own post saying RIP Henry because I didn't know what else to say.

Yasmin (Admin2)

Tuesday, 10 July, 01:35.

Afterlife

My comment had two hundred replies and over one hundred angry reactions. I read the first one or two comments before I deleted it.

I'm not religious but I don't like the idea of there being nothing after we die. Where's Henry now? His body is on a metal tray in a morgue somewhere but that isn't Henry. That's just a body.

I watched a documentary about morticians online. One of them said that even though the person is dead they are still patients until they leave the hospital for the funeral parlour.

I want to think Henry is with one of these people who still treat him like a human being.

Yasmin (Admin2)

Wednesday, 11 July, 01:28.
Last words

Dad's been asking me what happened at the party and I keep giving him the same answer. I don't know. I didn't take anything dodgy but I did down several tequila shots followed by vodka and coke. I've tried everything to remember but I can't, I swear I just can't. There's a black spot in my mind. I can remember parts. I remember setting the house up, I remember laughing with Megan and taking selfies with Chelsea. I remember Jake and his friends mucking about with their DJ stuff in the front room but I don't know if that was before or after the pictures.

I don't remember speaking to Henry but I think I must have at some point. What did Henry say to me? They could be his last fucking words. I thought for the long time that his last words to his mum were:

"I don't know. I won't be late back, I promise."

Because that's the last thing he'd written down about his mum. But that blog post was written a week before my party and he was bound to say something to her the next morning.

The more I think about Henry, the sicker I feel and if I think about it too hard I throw up. Dad caught me being sick just now and wanted to take me to the hospital but I told him I just wanted to sleep.

Yasmin (Admin2)

Wednesday, 11 July, 10.43.

Cards

The doorbell went around midday. I wasn't going to answer but someone kept tapping on the front room window and I couldn't ignore them.

Chelsea, Megan and Jake stood on the doorstep. Before I could say anything Megan flung her arms around me and started crying. 'I'm so sorry.'

She sunk of cigs. I felt her tear land on my neck as we hugged. It gave me goosebumps.

I pushed her towards Jake but when he didn't do anything Megan stepped into the house.

'Alright?' Jake asked me. His beard was unkempt and he looked like a tramp. I just nodded and let him through.

Chelsea gave me a hug as she came in.

'I don't really-' I was going to say want anyone over right now but Megan cut me off.

'You've cleaned up,' she said looking around the house.

'Well yeah, it was a fuckin' mess, wasn't it?' I don't think I'd ever seen the house cleaner, if I'm honest. I didn't know that the carpet was meant to be that colour. Dad had even wiped around the coffee stains on the table in the front room. 'It looks a lot better now it's clean and all.'

Things have been weird with Megan. She had a row with Jake because he wouldn't take her to prom. Megan then told us not to go so she wouldn't be alone but I told her to fuck off because I was looking forward to it.

'You got my DJ kit?' Jake asked.

'Nah. We had to throw it away.'

'What?'

'The police said we had to,' I lied.

Dad sprinted down the stairs, wearing his dressing gown. 'Were you three there?' he asked. 'What happened? Sit down.'

Chelsea, Megan and Jake glanced at each other.

'It's fuckin' shit, man,' Megan said, 'I can't believe he fuckin' died man. I mean, he was a good kid, an' all. Shit. It's shit isn't it, like really shit? What actually happened though?'

'What do you remember?' Dad said. He's never liked any of my friends. He'd hate them even more if he knew what they smoked.

'I woke up first. I went to the kitchen for a drink and everyone was still asleep. Then I saw Henry had been sick and then I saw his eyes were all weird and I - I screamed,' Megan said.

'It's fucked up,' Chelsea added.

Sick. I can remember the sick now. Henry was lying in a pool of his own sick.

'What about you?' Dad asked Chelsea. 'What do you know?

'Not a lot. Yas, what time did I get here?'

'Around eight.'

'Around eight, yeah. So I got here around eight and I helped with drinks and that was it really. I drank throughout the night and I slept over there, on a pile of coats.' Megan pointed to the kitchen doorway.

'And you?' Dad said to Jake. 'What did you do?'

'I was DJ-ing, I bought my kit and was DJ-ing throughout the night. Now it's gone. I've already spoken to the police, we all have but they didn't say anything about destroying my stuff.'

'Yeah. The police said we had to destroy it,' Dad said. 'Who brought the drugs?'

The three of them looked at each other before Jake answered, 'I knew there were drugs going around. Some of the people I spoke to were high in here but I didn't see who brought them.'

'Were any of you three... high?' Dad asked.

'Nah, man, nah, I never touch the stuff,' Jake said which I knew to be a blatant lie. When we were smoking in his car he was always talking about how baked he would get with his college friends.

'Out,' Dad said in almost a whisper. Megan and Chelsea stepped back but Jake didn't move.

'You're gonna pay me back for the DJ stuff, though, aren't you?'

'Fuck off, man,' I said. I was going to say something else but Jake was on his arse on the floor and Dad had gone apeshit.

'What did you say? What did you say?' he shouted. There was blood on his knuckles.

Megan squealed and sprinted for the door. Chelsea stood there, dumb and Jake practically shit himself as he legged it. I screamed, I couldn't stop staring at the blood. He'd hit Jake, he'd actually hit him.

Dad slammed the door behind my friends. 'You're not talking to them ever again, do you understand me?'

I was crying so much I couldn't say anything.

The letterbox clapped open and Megan's hand stuck an envelope through. I picked it up as Dad watched, through the front room window, my friends run down the street.

They gave me a card. It read: Sorry for your loss. Chelsea, Megan and Jake had written inside but I could hardly read their writing. I didn't know what to do with it so I gave it to Dad. He ripped it up without looking at it.

I honestly didn't know what to do, it was a shitty card but it was a nice thought. Dad started raging so I fled to my bedroom and put on my music.

Yasmin (Admin2)

Wednesday, 11 July, 11:04

Who gave Henry the drugs?

The police haven't told me anything. I spoke to an officer on the phone and quoted the case number but he said the investigation was ongoing. I still can't remember any more of what happened. Dad's stopped asking me because he knows he isn't going to get an answer. One thing keeps coming back to me though. Who gave Henry the drugs? I knew there were drugs at the party, I couldn't do anything about it though. I couldn't kick everyone out, could I? Who brought the drugs? Henry wouldn't use them by himself, he just wouldn't. Somebody encouraged him to or forced him too. Who?

Yasmin (Admin2)

Wednesday, 11 July, 13:57

Dean came over

I was in my room watching Netflix when my phone started buzzing. I ignored it but it kept buzzing for five minutes. Eventually I got so pissed off I answered.

'Who is it?'

'Babe, it's me. Let me in. I'm out front.'

Dad was in his study, I could hear the radio playing as I crept down the stairs. He had it tuned to a pop channel, they were playing "Cold Embrace."

"I wish you were mine, I wish I was told, you were a criminal, the best in the world."

The lyrics seemed to follow me to the front door. That's how Henry saw me, wasn't it?

Dean was waiting on his bike at the kerb.

'Hey,' he said. 'Alright?'

'You shouldn't be here,' I said, 'Dad went mental with the others.' I'm glad he's here though. Henry didn't know this but Dean's mum died when we were in year eleven. I was hoping Dean would know what to say.

'What the police been saying? They been back yet?'

'They want to speak to everyone at the party. They have the list from Facebook.'

'Shit,' he hissed.

'They not spoken to you yet?'

'Nah, they keep ringing and coming round but I've been staying out.'

'Where the fuck did you go afterwards?'

'I ain't gonna stay and speak to the police, am I? I went over the fence and along the track. I came out by the footbridge.'

'Right.'

'What did they say about Henry?'

'You've seen the article on Facebook?'

'Yeah but what did the police say to you?'

'Oh my god.'

Dean swore. 'You gotta tell me what-'

'Just listen, yeah? Did you bring anything to the party?'

'H-how can you even ask me that? Girl, I thought we were tight. You know that ain't me.'

'Look,' I almost told him that I'd had an abortion there and then. He does a right to know, it was his baby. But I couldn't say it.

'I was clean, bruv. Clean.'

'Whatever. You need to speak to the police.'

'Yeah I will, I will.' Dean put him helmet back on and revved his engine. 'I'll catch you later, yeah?'

I didn't bother saying anything and watched him race away.

Yasmin (Admin2)

Monday, 16 July, 19:36.

Summer School

I'd already mentioned Summer School to Dad before he went to Scotland and when he saw Chelsea leave a question on my Facebook wall asking if I was going, he wouldn't shut up about it.

'It'll do you good to get out of the house and see people again,' he kept saying 'but you have to stay away from people like Megan and Chelsea, do you understand me?'

The school was still open to the younger years, everyone would know about Henry. I purposely missed the bus so when I arrived late I could slip into the back of the assembly hall unnoticed. The hall was full, practically everyone in the year group was there. A rep from Stanlow University was droning on about student life, he looked about fifty and was backed by actual students from the uni. I sent Chelsea and Megan a joint text.

Me: I'm in the back row. Where R U?

I could feel those closest to me staring. The whispers that rippled around the hall might as well have been as loud as gunshots. I thought at least the teachers wouldn't give me agro but I could them gossiping from their places along the side of the hall. It makes sense though, they loved Henry too, everyone did. I flipped my hood up and tried to focus on the student rep. The band's equipment was out, as the rep paced up and down the hall, reading from his flashcards, he kept tripping over their wires.

When the rep had finished half an hour later Mrs Barton stepped forward.

'Thank you for that speech. All of the representatives from the other universities will be available in the common room for you to talk to. I highly recommend you do so.'

Chatter broke out which Mrs Barton silenced with a wave of her hand. My phone vibrated in my pocket.

Chelsea: Middle of the hall, right hand side.

I stood up in my seat to find the, and Mrs Barton spotted me, midsentence.

'University life is one of the – of course, I'm sure you're all aware of the dreadful event that happened several days ago. Henry Andrews from Mr Sandil's tutor group has sadly left us.'

Left us. That implies he had a choice, that it was his decision. Henry didn't choose to leave us, he was taken.

'We have a memorial in the Common Room. I suggest you all visit and pay your respects. As I'm sure you know Henry died of a drug overdose. We've invited several charities and organisations to speak about the danger of drugs and to raise awareness for the causes.'

I felt those nearest turn to look at me.

'Henry's funeral will be Thursday. The procession will pass by the school at half past nine. Everyone will be invited out to the field to watch Henry pass.'

Mrs Barton told everyone to go to the Common Room to speak to the reps. I was sitting nearest to the door and left the hall before anyone could talk to me. I paced down the corridor to the Common Room, hoping everyone would be distracted and I could find Chelsea and Megan when they arrived.

The first thing I saw in the Common Room was a banner that read DRUG ADDICTION CAN KILL. It belonged to a charity that had set up a stall by the settees. Half the Common Room was dedicated to charities about drugs and depression, the other half was for universities and colleges. Henry's picture from photo day had been set up on a desk in the middle of the room. Some idiot had lit candles around the picture and people had been leaving their messages on a whiteboard at the front of the desk. Henry's Facebook wall had over two hundred messages.

As the year group crammed into the Common Room I heard one of the reps say to another, 'Who's the picture of?'

'No idea, some kid that OD'ed.'

Henry had become a school legend.

I saw Henry's mum at the far side of the room talking to Joe, Adam and Mrs Barton. All four of them were crying.

Mrs Barton looked across the room, saw me and began to forge a path through the crowd.

I ran.

Jake wasn't waiting outside the school with his car so I didn't have our regular smoking hut. I sat down on the kerb and rolled a cigarette. When Chelsea and Megan arrived I'd already finished my third.

'Alright?' Megan asked.

I grunted. 'Dean not there?' I asked, nodding back to the school.

Chelsea shrugged, 'Not seen him.'

'Jake?' I asked.

'Broke up,' Megan said.

I didn't ask why they broke up because at that exact moment I couldn't care less but Megan decided to tell me anyway.

'It's because of Dean actually. When he couldn't find his keys to his bike to go to Thorpe Park he found us smoking in Jake's car and ordered Jake to drive him there. Jake said no because he had to get back to college. They had a fight and Dean broke one of the wing mirrors on the car. Jake was so pissed off that he kicked us out the car and took it straight to the garage. He was such a stress head. He's still going on about his broken DJ stuff, as well.'

We spent most of day out on the pavement gossiping and smoking in the sun. Chelsea convinced me to go back inside for the final hour of the day. She said that the reps from Stanlow Uni were really fit and it was getting too hot outside. I think she secretly wanted to learn more about University life which is fair enough. She's probably the only one of us going to University, anyway.

We found everyone back in the assembly hall. The band were tuning their instruments.

We took our seats in the back row, unnoticed, as Will said into the mic, 'This song is for Henry,' Lots of bands write songs about people that have died but Will was a terrible singer and the band played their instruments too loudly to hear what was being sung. Everyone clapped at the end of the song and the band looked as if they had just played at fucking Wembley Arena or something.

Yasmin (Admin2)

Tuesday, 17 July, 02:14

Adam and Joe

Dad wanted me to go the second day at Summer School. He was super stressed about it so I went along just to make him happy.

I didn't know what to do when I got to school, all of the Sixth formers were in classrooms listening to university lecturers so I wandered down the corridors nobody uses.

I kept thinking how Henry had walked down these corridors unaware of what was going to happen to him. It sounds so stupid but it's true. Thousands of students have walked up and down these corridors and Henry was just another one of them. I kept thinking how Henry wouldn't stand out and how unfair it was that out of all of those students Henry was the one who suffered when he was the one who least deserved it. My thoughts kept returning to how no one will miss him. That made me really angry and I couldn't do anything apart from walk so I just got more pissed off.

I was passing by an open classroom door when a voice said, 'Nah, Henry wouldn't have done that.'

I stopped. It was an old computer classroom. Adam and Joe were sitting near the door. They were so engrossed in their computer screens that they didn't notice me.

'Would he though?' Joe said. 'He might have done. He might have wanted to see what it was like, you know?'

'Have you ever?' Adam asked.

'Nah.'

'But would you?

Joe glanced up from his computer and saw me.

'You two alright?' I asked, trying to keep my voice steady.

'Yeah, we're cool,' Adam said. He eyed Joe, who said after a pause,

'Yeah. We're fine,'

I peered around the room. They had it to themselves, the computers were old and I'm talking thick screens old. Still, it wouldn't be past Adam and Joe to use a proxy server to play games, browse Facebook and do whatever.

'Is this where you went with Henry?' I asked.

'What?'

'Henry was always taking about going to a computer room with you guys, away from everywhere else.' All I knew about the computer room was what Henry had written on this blog.

'Yeah,' Adam said, 'this is it.'

'It's nice.'

'What else did Henry say?' Joe asked.

'Huh?'

'What else did Henry say about us?'

'He said... he said he really liked you two.' I didn't know what to say.

'That's it?'

'Is that it? Yeah, that's it. That's what he said.' I didn't have the energy to keep calm.

Joe's fist clenched and I darted out of reach as he sprang from his chair and barreled towards me.

Don't get me wrong, I could have beaten both of these boys in a fight. I've had Karate lessons since I was six and I really wanted to hurt someone.

But not them.

I sidestepped Joe and then pushed Adam back into the IT room before he could do anything stupid.

Joe charged at me again, arms raised out like a zombie, screaming, mouth literally foaming like a rabid dog.

'You fucking killed him!'

I stuck out my leg sidestepped Joe once again. He face planted on the corridor floor, his glasses skidding under a fire extinguisher.

'Calm down, dickhead,' I said. Joe had reached the point where you're so angry you can't do anything. He screamed, snatched up his glasses and sprinted down the corridor.

Adam shouted after him.

'Adam,' I said, 'he won't-'

Adam blanked me and chased after his friend.

I spent the next hour hiding in the girl's toilets, like a fucking year seven, crying. The bell for end of lesson one sounded and the corridors swarmed with students but no one found me. I didn't want to stay in school and I couldn't go home. I wanted to go somewhere else. Anywhere else. I texted Megan and Chelsea but they didn't answer. Chelsea wouldn't want to be pulled out of Summer School a second time. I'm glad Megan didn't answer, I felt she would only annoy me by talking about Jake.

I waited ten minutes to ensure the corridors were quiet before I opened the stall door. I've bunked school tons of times, there are millions of way to do it. The first is through reception, our student cards mean we can simply buzz through the door. The risk is the receptionist will be watching and anyone could be waiting in reception. Option two is to climb over the school gate. This is where the smokers hang out and didn't want to be seen. That leaves option three, the school fence. It's easy enough to climb over you just need to find a quiet spot.

I ran through the school and didn't see anyone until I skirted around the edge of the field searching for a low point in the fence.

'Yasmin.'

Mrs Barton stood on the pavement, a cigarette dangling between in her fingers.

'Fuck off.' I started to climb.

'Yasmin, look at me.'

'Fuck off.' I swung over the top of the fence and landed on the pavement beside her. I walked away but I could hear her keeping pace with me.

'Yasmin, if you go home I will follow you.'

'Yeah?'

'Yasmin, look at me.' She snatched onto my hoodie but I didn't have it zipped up. I shrugged out of it and ran.

I bought a box of ciggies in Sainsbury's and sat on their car park wall for a couple hours, watching the traffic pass on the high street. Mrs Barton would have called my dad so

I knew he'd be waiting for me at home. I honestly wouldn't be surprised if she kept my hoodie. Bitch.

I was there for a couple of hours, burning through my cigs. I was wondering if I could get Mrs Barton done for physical assault when a tin can struck the wall next to me.

Henry's mum stood in the middle of the carpark. Her eyes were red and raw like a meth addict's. She was shaking, like Joe had been shaking in the IT room. Several carrier bags lay by her feet, the contents spilling out onto the tarmac.

I didn't have time to say anything.

'You bitch,' she shrieked. She snatched another tin of dog food from the ground. I vaulted over the carpark wall, the tin skimmed my shoulder and struck a parked car, sounding the alarm.

I didn't stop running until I reached the bus stop.

Yasmin (Admin2)

Tuesday, 17 July, 22:22.
Stealing wine

I haven't told Dad about Henry's mum in the carpark, he was already furious about Mrs Barton. She phoned him before I got home. I don't want to write about the argument here but at the end of it we were both crying.

I spent the next day in my room where I finished Gatsby and kept rereading Henry's posts. I kept thinking about how much I wanted to get drunk and pretend that none of this had happened. I'd already emptied Dad's drink cupboard so I slipped downstairs and snuck out to the corner shop.

The cashier raised her eyebrows at me when I put a bottle of wine on her counter.

'ID?' she asked.

'Lost it.'

'I can't serve you without ID.'

'Can't you just take the change from the twenty instead? Y'know?'

She shook her head and I saw her reach under the counter to call a bell for assistance. I snatched the bottle and ran out.

I opened the bottle back in my room but it smelled like shit. I've had to put my music on, I can hear Dad crying from his study.

Yasmin (Admin2)

Tuesday, 17 July, 23:03.
Drinking the wine

The wine tastes as bad as it smells.

Yasmin (Admin2)

Wednesday, 18 July, 12:25.

Death by misadventure

I woke up to the voice of Sergeant Rickman talking to Dad downstairs. I couldn't hear what that being said but I managed to catch the words "wine" and "camera".

'Yasmin,' Sergeant Rickman said when I came downstairs. He was accompanied by a female office who had the body of a rugby player.

'My name is Sergeant Terrell. I'm also a counselor,' the woman said.

Dad turned into a stuttering idiot and raced away to the kitchen to pour everyone a drink. I eyed the leaflets Sergeant Terrell was holding titled The Dangers of Drugs.

'How are you feeling, Yasmin?' Sergeant Terrell asked me.

'Fine. I don't need to see a sodding counselor.'

Before she could say anything Dad chose that moment to return with drinks.

'We're still trying to trace everyone at your party to take a statement,' Sergeant Rickman said, 'and there's a few people we can't get hold of.' He listed several names but I didn't recognize any of them.

'Might be friends of my boyfriend,' I said. 'Have you asked him?'

'Not yet. We've had trouble contacting him. Can you ring him for us and ask him to come over?'

I rang Dean's mobile but he didn't answer.

'The coroner has ruled Henry's death as accidental,' Sergeant Rickman said, 'death by misadventure. The toxicologist's report says Henry died of an overdose from a drug called Rose. Are you familiar with it?'

'Are you asking me if I've ever taken any?' I could feel Dad staring at me. 'No.'

I haven't but I've always wanted to see what it was like, what the fuss was about.

'Do you know who supplied that drug at your party?'

'I've already told you this. I don't know.'

'So you don't know who gave him the drug?' I asked, 'because Henry wouldn't smoke it by himself.'

'Yasmin,' Dad snapped.

'Everyone at the party was either too drunk or high to remember,' Sergeant Terrell said, 'Unless you've remembered anything else?'

She looked at me expectantly as though I was about to reveal something that will crack the fucking case.

'Henry wouldn't smoke the drug.'

The two officers look at each other and Dad had the nerve to say, 'Please Yasmin, try and think.'

'What do you fuckin' think I've been trying to do?'

'Calm down,' Sergeant Rickman said, 'Try to think clearly.'

I only did what he said because I was worried he would arrest me in my own house. Wouldn't everyone at school love that?

I retold the events of that night. Chelsea and Megan arrived first. Then Jake and his friends. Then Dean and his friends. Then Henry. People sort of appeared and disappeared throughout the night, I didn't keep track of them. I couldn't remember what in what order things had happened. Selfies with the girls, someone riding my bike around the garden, one of Dean's friends puking up. Sergeant Terrell jotted down notes and interrupted me throughout with stupid questions.

'Is Dean your ex-boyfriend?' she asked.

'Yeah. We were still friends.'

I admitted to going upstairs with Dean and I told them about seeing Henry in the front room on his phone.

'I didn't come down until the next morning when Megan told me no one could wake up Henry.'

'Was Dean with you the whole night?' Sergeant Rickman asked.

'Yeah.'

'Did you have sexual intercourse?'

Dad took a sharp intake of breath as I answered, 'yeah.'

The police interviewed me for another hour and threatened to take me back to the station at one point when I told them I didn't know what more they wanted of me. They asked the same questions over and over again hoping I would change my answers and make their job easier. I stuck with my version of the truth.

'We received reports of you shoplifting yesterday evening,' Sergeant Rickman said. 'The cashier says you stole a bottle of wine.'

I was so pissed off that I didn't care what happened at that point. 'Yeah, that was me,' I said.

Dad looked as though he had been punched in the stomach.

'You gave the shop assistant quite a fright,' Sergeant Rickman said. 'She's going off with stress.'

'Christ, it was only one bottle.'

Dad excused himself and went upstairs. Pussy.

'Given the recent events and the stress you're under we're going to give you an official warning. Do you understand?' Sergeant Rickman asked.

'Yeah.'

'You have to understand that it's very unlikely charges will be brought forward for Henry's death.'

I didn't answer that. Then they gave their little speech about counselling and Sergeant Terrell gave me her contact details. As I was showing them out Dad came back downstairs clutching the empty wine bottle from my room.

'Do you want to take this?' he asked, 'as evidence?'

'Dad, what the fuck?'

Sergeant Rickman looked at Sergeant Terrell who nodded and fetched an evidence bag from the car.

'Jesus Christ, Yasmin,' Dad said when they left. 'Your Mother would-' I was going to shout at Dad but he started blubbering. A fully grown man, crying. Pathetic.

Yasmin (Admin2)

Wednesday, 18 July, 19:08

No more smoking

I've been in my room all day and refused to speak to Dad. He hasn't knocked on my door to apologise either.

Out of my window I could see Henry's mum in her garden with around twenty people. My first thought was it was the wake of Henry's funeral. Everyone was dressed in black and lots of candles had been placed everywhere. I think I saw Henry's Uncle Patrick there but I don't know him that well so I'm not sure. I spotted Wilfred though, darting between everyone's legs.

Henry's mum was reading from a card to her guests. I was reminded of a poem you would read at a funeral. I like poems. I used to write them all the time in primary school. There's a new thing now called spoken word which is a mixture of rap and poetry. I wonder if Henry knew about it, he would have liked it.

I tried to google a poem for Henry's funeral. I wasn't going to read it out or anything like that but I thought if Henry's mum choose a crap poem, and she would, I could think of my better one. I couldn't find a poem I thought was strong enough for Henry. In the end, I tried to write my own. I sat at my desk for a good twenty minutes trying to think of something to write but I gave up and rolled a cigarette.

I watched the gathering from my window as I smoked, half hoping they wouldn't see me and half hoping they would and invite me over. Then I remembered that Mrs Barton has said the funeral was tomorrow and this couldn't be the wake. Some people have a pre-wake or a private goodbye, maybe that's what Henry's family were doing?

I reached for another cigarette but knocked the box off my window sill. It bounced off the back fence and landed beside the tracks. I thought about the cigarettes I smoked when I was pregnant. I'd tried cutting down but I found it too hard. I'd felt drained without them, dead inside. Like how I felt now.

I noticed that it was a starless sky and thought about the phrase Henry used when we were on the footbridge together. Despite the people below me it did feel like an Empty Night.

I thought about the cigarettes I gave Henry after the music gig and the scent of nicotine in my room suddenly seemed stronger.

I need to find out who killed Henry. He didn't deserve to die, it's not fair. I need to know who gave Henry the Rose.

I want to stop smoking.

Yasmin (Admin2)

Thursday, 19 July, 21:38.
Henry's funeral

At 09:15 the school tannoy went off. It was Mrs Barton.

Mrs Barton: Could all students please assemble on the school field. Thank you.

We didn't march out to the school field in silence like you would see in a film. People went out there, laughing and chatting. I wanted to smack every single one of them. Henry hadn't been popular but by this point everyone in school had heard of him. That kid who OD'ed. Even those who knew him like Adam and Joe didn't walk in silence like they should have done.

The field was wide enough to have everyone stand in a row but of course they all stood in little groups gossiping. The teachers stood behind the students and, I won't lie, I was happy to see some of them crying. Mrs Barton was crying with Adam and Joe. Bethany elbowed Will to be quiet. Chelsea and Megan stood near me, close enough to talk to me, but far enough away to deny actually being with me. Dean wasn't there. I'd happily swap his life for Henry's. I know death doesn't work like that and I know I sound like a complete twat but that's what I think.

I'm not sure what the plan was between Henry's mum and the school but it took ages for the hearse to appear. When it finally rolled into view, I choked. The hearse was basically a glass box on wheels with a black coffin in the middle. It was drawn by two black horses and there was a bouquet of flowers propped against the coffin that read SON. I don't know if they were from Henry's mum or dad but I spotted his mum in the limo following the hearse. She was crying, obviously, and waved to us as she passed. I spotted Henry's dad in the car behind her. He wasn't crying yet but you could tell he was going to. There were seven cars in total which surprised me because I didn't realise Henry's family was so big.

Some of the kids cried as the procession rolled past. One year seven kid even removed his hat. I don't know if he was being serious or not. Then it was over. The last car rounded the bend towards the high street and they were gone. The students began to wander back to the school as the bell for first lesson rang.

I dawdled at the back of the crowd until everyone had reached the school. Then I sprinted into reception, buzzed my way through the door and ran to the bushes in the car park where I'd stashed my bike.

I was so focused on reaching the carpark that I didn't hear the person following me. Then something struck me in the back of the head and I tumbled to the ground.

'You... stupid... bitch...' a female voice panted.

I leaped to my feet as my attacker charged towards me, arms flailing. I panicked, stuck out my fist and the person ran straight into it. They collided into me and we both rolled across the tarmac.

Grace screamed. I've had nothing to do with Grace before, I've hardly spoken to her. I knew she fancied Henry but Jesus Christ.

'Calm down and shut up,' I hissed but Grace screamed again . Then she spat in my face.

She spat in my face.

I was so disgusted that I lost my grip on her.

'You killed him,' she screeched.

'I didn't-'

'You fucking killed him.'

'Calm it, bitch.' I grabbed her by the hair and forced her to her knees.

'Listen to me,' I said. 'I didn't kill Henry, alright? Someone gave him a drug and he had a bad reaction to it. I didn't give him the drug, ok? It wasn't me.'

Grace wasn't listening. I pushed her to the ground and snatched up my bike.

I thought that would be the end of it. I didn't think of Grace as a fighter but she kicked out and her foot connected with my front tyre. I toppled off from my bike.

'Murderer,' Grace bellowed.

I blinked dirt out of my eye and wiped away the blood under my nose.

Grace faltered. She stood there, frozen in place, too scared to move. Maybe it was the sight of blood or maybe her courage had left her.

But it wasn't her fault she was angry. To her credit, she only started crying when I cycled away.

When I reached the road towards the high street I couldn't see the procession. I didn't know what cemetery they planned to bury Henry in, I had planned to leave school quickly so I wouldn't lose sight of them.

The street was silent now that everyone had returned to the classrooms. I saw a flash of orange at the end of the road as a car turned onto the high street.

Mr Roth's car.

When I reached the high street Mr Roth was already half way down the road. Ahead of him, stopped at a traffic light was the funereal.

The lights changed.

I kicked off from the kerb and peddled down the middle of the high street weaving in and out of traffic and ignoring the pedestrians I almost knocked over. Even though the funeral wasn't going to outrace me I still want to be close to Henry. I was almost level with Mr Roth when it happened. Out of nowhere, this car appeared from a side turning by the library. My traffic light was red but that old woman wasn't looking where she was going. Her front bumper hit my rear tyre and I went flying off my bike for the second time. I collided with the back of Mr Roth's car, smashing his brake light and jarring my shoulder.

The woman leaped out of her car, brandishing a walking stick but before I could do anything Mr Roth was standing next to me, shouting back at her. I don't remember what he said to her but she got back in her car and drove away.

'What the hell do you think you're doing?'

I grimaced and climbed to my feet.

'Christ, you could have been killed. Imagine how Henry's family would have felt.'

'I doubt I would have bloody died.' The back wheel of my bike was bent out of shape.

'Don't swear at me,' Mr Roth said. 'Get in.'

'You understand I could be fired for this,' he said as we left the high street and followed the procession. 'Giving a student a lift in my car.'

'I won't tell anyone.'

'That's not the point.'

I was scared he would turn around and take me back to school but when it became obvious he wasn't going to I started to relax.

I'd dumped my bike at the side of the road. There's was no room for it in Mr Roth's car and it was useless anyway, the back wheel was fucked. My jeans had ripped around the knees and my right shoulder flared in pain whenever I moved it. I used the mirror in the passenger's windshield to wipe the blood from my face.

We followed the funeral in silence until we reached the church. It wouldn't have looked out of place in a horror film, the spires were black and seemed to be attempting to cut into the clouds.

The coffin was already being carried inside.

Mr Roth swore and swung the car into a parking spot. I leapt out leaving the passenger door open and ran towards the church, ignoring his shouts.

I slipped into the back row and picked up an order of service as the coffin bearers reached their seats. Henry's coffin had been placed on a trestle at the front of the church. This was the closest I had been to him since the party. The church was packed, standing room only. I spotted Henry's mum and dad in the front row and Henry's dad's girlfriend behind them. She was dressed like it was a Big Brother Eviction night. I recognised some of the people I had seen in Henry's garden including his Uncle Patrick.

A vicar stood before us, he opened his arms and said, 'I'm glad you could join us today for the funeral of Henry Andrews. Please be seated.'

Mr Roth joined me as the first hymn started. Henry wasn't religious so I don't know why it started with a hymn. I couldn't stop thinking that Henry wouldn't have wanted this. He wouldn't want any religious songs. After the first hymn the vicar thanked us all for coming and told us about Henry, as though we didn't know whose funeral it was. After the second hymn Henry's mum went to the front of the church.

'Thank you all for coming, Henry would have been very grateful. Henry was an inspiration for everyone who knew him. They say the brightest star burns half as long and maybe Henry wasn't-' But she couldn't say anymore. Uncle Patrick had to help her back to her seat.

I ended up crying away at the back of the church. The worst part was when the last hymn ended and the curtains started to close, separating us from Henry.

'What you did today was very dangerous,' Mr Roth said as we walked back to his car.

I nodded. I couldn't be arsed with an argument. It was easier to let him think I was sorry.

'You could have been killed, for Christ's sake.'

He stared at me as I sat in the passenger seat. 'Yasmin, are you listening to me?'

'Yeah,' I deadpanned. 'You're saying what I did was very stupid.'

'Yes and don't even think of doing something like that again. Do you understand?'

When I didn't answer he swore and drove me back to the school.

Yasmin (Admin2)

Friday, 20 July, 01:13.
The Supplier

I tried to find the Facebook event for my party but the police must have deleted it. I didn't know everyone who was invited, so I've messaged the ones I do remember and asked them to share my message on. I messaged fifty people asking if they spoke to Henry, if they know who the supplier was or if they saw anything suspicious to speak to me.

When I clicked back on the messages an hour later ten people had already blocked me.

Yasmin (Admin2)

Friday, 20 July, 13:29.

Seeing the school counselor

I've never had anything to do with Mrs Saunders before. I knew who she was, the student counselor. I was meant to have meetings with her about me missing school but I never turned up to any of them. The only things I knew about her was from what I'd read on Henry's blog.

Like Henry said, her office was decorated with these really cringy motivation posters.

Always set a trail, never follow a path.

Direct actions gets the goods.

Believe in tomorrow because it is a brand new day.

That kind of crap.

Mrs Saunders smiled when I arrived and asked me to take a seat, 'How are you feeling after everything that happened, Yasmin?' she asked.

'I'm fine.'

'Really? Losing someone close to you it one of the hardest things a person can go through.'

I shrugged.

'You could have come and seen me sooner. My door is open to everyone. Technically you're still a student here until you collect your results. You have to understand that what happened to Henry isn't your fault. You know that, don't you?'

I stared her out. She sounded like a priest. How often had Henry come here? What had he talked about with her?

'Sometimes… bad things happen. It isn't fair but death is a part of life.'

Christ, she sounded like the posters on her wall.

'How do you feel your exams went?' Mrs Saunders asked.

'Crap probably.' I hadn't walked out of any of my exams like Dean but I know I failed them all. I doubt I did well in geography, despite Henry's help.

'Why do you say that?' She jotted something down in a notepad.

I shrugged and adjusted myself on the chair.

'Do you mind if I ask how things are at home?'

'Everythin' at home's fine.'

'Hmm.. and what are you plans now? After Sixth form?'

'Dunno yet. I've not really thought abou' it.'

'Back in term time I spoke to everyone about their options after school. Have you thought about college or maybe staying in Sixth form for another year?'

'I don't wanna stay here.'

As she looked at me I could see her examine the cuts and scrapes on my body. I had tried to hide the bruising with makeup. I leant in my chair to see what she was writing.

Self harm? Postpartum depression?

She knew. She knew about my pregnancy and knew about my abortion. I thought about all the ways she'd asked Henry if there was anything he wanted to tell her. She'd wanted to know more about me. 'You've been seeing Henry,' I stated. 'You've been having meetings with him all year.'

'Y-yes, I have.'

'What did he say to you?' I asked.

Mrs Saunders put down her notepad. 'Yasmin I don't think-' I had already stopped listening. I eyed her notepad and then the drawers under her desk. If Henry had been having meetings with her, surely Mrs Saunders would have a file on him?

There was a thump on the door. The cries of "fight, fight, fight, fight" caused Mrs Saunders to spring from her chair. Two year seven students were wrestling on the floor, circled by their friends. I swear, it was like a really lame version of Fight Club. While Mrs Saunders was distracted I dived for the drawers.

Locked.

'I've gotta go.'

'Yasmin, wait you-'

I slipped past her, pushed through the year seven's and ran down the corridor as more teachers arrived.

Yasmin (Admin2)

Friday, 20 July, 16:42.
Breaking in

I don't know why Henry was seeing a psychologist and counselor but whatever the reason it would be written down in Henry's file. Henry's file can also tell me if he was mentally unstable or depressed or whatever which would explain why he smoked the Rose. I need to know. I just do, I owe it to Henry to find out what happened to him. He deserves that. Not knowing makes me want to punch something.

Mrs Saunders knew about my pregnancy but she couldn't say anything. If she did it would have spooked Henry, he would have deleted the blog and mentally nosedived. Who else knows? That Dr West bloke for one. He would have read everything.

Although Sixth form has finished, Summer School finishes today. I can walk into school at three, wait until Mrs Saunders is out of her office and then break in and steal the file. The only question is how to open her locked office door and locked drawers.

I've checked, Dad has a screwdriver set downstairs.

I caught the bus to school and spent half an hour in the Common Room, chilling on the computers. Henry's shrine had been dismantled but I was happy to see that people had been etching his names into the desks. The sad fact is that these cuts will last a lot longer than the memory of Henry will.

When the bell for the end of the school day sounded I watched everyone leave. Ten minutes later Mrs Barton's office light went off. I waited another two minutes and crept to the door. At the start of the term Dean had crept into her office to steal back his phone that Mrs Barton had confiscated. Although Mrs Barton had caught him, Dean told me that she kept forgetting to lock her office door.

Mrs Barton's desk was covered with papers and unmarked homework. I sat in her chair and searched through each draw until I found her keys. I didn't want to stay too long in case she came back. I spotted a business card on her desk.

Doctor West. Psychologist and counselor.

I had a quick look for my hoodie as well but it wasn't there.

The corridor to Mrs Saunders' office was empty but I could see her coat and handbag inside, she couldn't be far away. Legally she had to lock her door because of the confidential documents she kept. It took me five minutes to find the right key.

I used Dad's screwdriver set to pry open the draws. It took me ten minutes and not going to lie, it's the closest I ever felt to being a spy.

The paperwork was in folders, with the student's name written on each in black marker pen. I flicked through the names until I found H, Andrews. I didn't take the paperwork out of the office. I laid it out on the floor, and took a picture of each page on my phone. Then I put the papers back in the folder and back in drawer. It wasn't stealing, it's only breaking and entering.

The office door opened. A year seven boy stood in the doorway, paralysed. His eyes were red, I think he was one of Mrs Saunders' regulars.

'Miss?' He said looking down the corridor.

'Fuckin' move.' I barged pasted him, knocking the poor sod over. I can honestly say that I've never been so scared in my life. Mrs Saunders screamed when she saw me sprinting towards her but I darted past and kept running.

Dad was waiting at the front door.

It must have shown on my face that I'd really fucked up. He slammed the front door and started yelling, demanding to know why I had broken into the school. I tried to walk away but he followed me around the house then his screwdriver fell out of my pocket We only stopped screaming at each other when there was a flash of blue outside the front room windows and a knock at the door.

I watched through the windows as Dad opened the front door to Sergeant Rickman and Sergeant Terrell.

'We're looking for Yasmin,' I heard Sergeant Terrell said. 'Is she in?'

'Oh Christ.'

He led them into the front room to me. I laid down on the settee and tried to act casual as Dad lead the police officers to me.

'Hey,' I grinned. It probably looked more like a smirk.

'Yasmin,' Sergeant Rickman stated.

'Yeah?'

'Jesus, oh Jesus,' Dad muttered.

That killed me, it really did.

'Where were you about an hour ago?' Sergeant Terrell asked.

'Out,' I said.

'Out where?'

'Just out and about.'

Dad swore again.

'We have reason to believe you were vandalising Norcrest Academy,' Sergeant Terell said.

'Do you have any proof?' I asked.

'Fuck,' Dad said. 'fuck, fuck, Yasmin oh my – fuck.'

The only other time I'd seen Dad freak out like this was when Mum died.

I didn't get arrested in the end. Fuck knows how. They took me down to the police station and showed me the footage from a security camera. It had watched me unlock Mrs Saunders' office. Sergeant Terrell said that because of the recent events she doubted the school would prosecute me but it would be up to them if they wanted to press charges. I overheard Sergeant Rickman telling Dad that he doubted the school would.

Dad didn't speak to me on the drive home. He only started to shout when we got inside.

'What the fuck were you doing?'

'I hate that place.'

'They could've have expelled you.'

'Nah, they wouldn't have done. They ain't got the balls. I've finished there anyway,' I said knowing there was a chance I may have to re-sit a year.

'You don't think, do you Yasmin? You just don't fucking think.'

'How do you know what I think? You stay in your fucking study all day. All you do is moan like a fuckin' manchild.'

'Yasmin that is enough. When you have a family, you'll see what-'

'You don't even know what I've... Dad listen to me, yeah? I had an abortion. I had it two months ago.'

Dad's mouth opened but he couldn't form the words he wanted. 'w-wh-'

'I had an abortion Dad. It was Dean's. He doesn't know.'

Yasmin (Admin2)

Saturday, 21 July, 03:22.

The moment I knew I was pregnant

My period was late. I clocked on why during the school trip to the factory. I bought myself a pregnancy test in Boots and nipped into the bushes at the riverside because I needed to know then and there wasn't anywhere else to go. Dean wouldn't leave me alone so I had to have a go at him so he would bugger off. Then I did the test.

Positive. Pregnant.

It's the only test I've ever fucking passed.

Of course I did another test when I got home, just to be sure but it said positive too. I'd woken up feeling ill tons of time recently but I thought they were just hangovers.

Henry was right when he said two other girls become pregnant while we were at Norcrest but I didn't know either of them. The first was a year ten girl who became pregnant the first time she had sex. When her boyfriend found out, he legged it. His whole family moved house and after a while the girl moved away too. The second girl was in the year above me. She was a nutcase and planned her pregnancy so she could marry her boyfriend or some crazy crap.

I've not told Dean about my pregnancy for the same reason I couldn't tell Dad. I was scared. Henry was right when he wrote, Dean has a right to know. Dean would kill me for not telling him about it and would have absolutely no interest in having a child with me but he should still know.

Yasmin (Admin2)

Saturday, 21 July, 14:26.

Henry's file

I tried to read Henry's file last night but I was too tired and I couldn't understand it. I went to bed at half three. When I woke up I could hear two voices downstairs. The first's was Dad, but I couldn't make out who he was talking to. My first thought was Sergeant Rickman again but when I crept on the landing it was obvious it wasn't him. The voice was familiar but I couldn't place it.

'-always out,' I heard Dad say, 'and when's she here, she's always in her room.'

'I've spoken to our counselor and she's recommended a support group.'

'Yeah, the police officers said the same.'

The stairs creaked as I tried to creep down.

'Yasmin, there's someone here for you,' Dad called.

I swore and came down the stairs.

'Yasmin,' Mrs Barton said as though I had just stepped into her office. I remembered her saying she would come to my house but I didn't think she would actually do it. She was wearing a summer dress as though she was going for a picnic in a park or something. I was in my pajamas.

'What are you doing here?'

'Yasmin, don't be so rude,' Dad snapped. 'Would you like another drink, Betty?'

'Only if Yasmin is having one,' Mrs Barton said cringing at the sound of her first name. The name Betty Barton sounds like a comic book character.

Dad disappeared into the kitchen and I noticed several empty tea cups on the table. How long had they been sitting here gossiping about me?

'We didn't finish our chat the other day,' Mrs Barton said. I could hear the smugness in her voice.

'This is for you.' She held out a plastic carrier bag. I reached inside and pulled out my hoodie.

'I suppose you want to know what happened as well?' I asked.

'I'm here to tell you that the school isn't going to press

charges and the Mrs Saunders' desk has been fixed.'

I grunted.

'Yasmin, that was a very stupid thing to do, breaking into the school.'

'Fuck off.'

Dad shouted from the kitchen but I ignored him.

'Listen to me,' Mrs Barton said, 'I'm sorry. You must understand that and I expect you're tired of hearing it from everyone but I am. I'm so sorry. The student council has approved a bench to be made in memory of Henry.'

'A bench? And how long till someone etches into it?'

Mrs Barton didn't answer. She closed her eyes as though preparing herself.

'Yasmin. What's been going on? You've missed most of the school year.'

'None of your fucking business.'

'Yasmin, I am not your enemy. I gave you the ticket for Thorpe Park, do you remember?'

When she gave me her ticket at Thorpe Park she said, 'you might as well take it, then.' It wasn't a peace offering or anything like that. It's the same reason she didn't kick me off the coach. She only discovered me after we'd left the school and she didn't have the energy to argue with me, she knew I'll cause a fuss.

'Did you go to the funereal?' I spat.

'No. No one from the school did. I felt it wouldn't be appropriate.'

I almost shouted that I was there but stopped myself. That would lead to awkward questions and I didn't want to drop Mr Roth in the shit.

'Yasmin, you are not the only one hurting. Henry's mum is seeing doctors to cope, I've had Joe and Adam in my office-'

'Do you even know what the drug was called that killed 'im?'

'Yasmin, I don't have to answer to you.'

'I'm not a student anymore, you can't do shit. What was the name of the drug that killed Henry, do you know?'

Mrs Barton glared at me.

'It's called Rose. We both know Henry wouldn't use drug, don't we? We know someone tricked him and gave it to him. Who do you think it was, then?

'Why?'

'What do you mean, why?'

'Yasmin, knowing who gave Henry the drug won't bring him back. It won't make a difference. He could have chosen to taken it himself.'

'Screw you, Betty. We both know he wouldn't, don't we?'

Dad came hurrying back into the room but Betty was already on her feet. 'Perhaps I'll come back another time.'

As Dad apologised I shoved passed them and held the front door open.

I had another argument with Dad which involved both of us crying and me throwing one of the tea cups against a wall where it smashed but I don't want to go into the details of that. Henry's password is pissing me off.

Norcrest. Skyrim. Manu. Man united. Arsenal.

I gave up and typed up Henry's report from the pictures on my phone. I still don't understand most of it but I think I found what I was looking for.

"Henry is a shy child of average build in his final year of Sixth form at Norcrest academy. Henry has no abnormal violent issues.

Henry has struggled academically but has attempted all of his classes to the best of his ability. Despite this and his high attendance Henry has yet to make a choice for life after Norcrest. He has applied for an English course but lacks enthusiasm.

Henry has little foresight for the future and what he wishes to achieve after education. He is aiming for straight C's in all of his subject as he believes it will reward him with enough UCAS points to leave him with several options. Henry has suffered in the past with social and mental issues although these seems to have de-escalated. Henry admits to spending most of his break and lunch times in a disused IT room with a close circle of friends."

Henry was over his mental problems. He didn't smoke the drug willingly.

Yasmin (Admin2)

Sunday, 22 July, 18:27.

Debrief

I had a text from Mistveil clinic almost immediately after I published that last post. It was a reminder text about my debrief session which I've just had.

I don't like the term debrief. It makes it sound like removing the fetus from my womb had been a military mission and this was the victory talk. I wanted to go, so I could have that whole damn thing done with.

I felt sorry for not telling Dad this big event was happening in my life so I asked him if he wanted to drive me to the clinic for my final session.

I met the two Doctors who had seen me for the operation they lead me into the surgery room with Dad. They asked me how I was getting on.

'Fine,' I lied as I took off my hoodie.

'Are you sure?' asked the first doctor.

'No. My friend... the one who brought me here for the treatment. He died.'

'Oh,' the second Doctor said, 'I'm so sorry. The boy who waited outside?'

I nodded. Dad glanced out of the window at the car park and the bins where Henry had waited.

After the session the first Doctor said, 'The good news is that everything here is finished. You won't have to return, although if you experience any discomfort or bleeding you need to let us know, okay?'

They then asked Dad if they could tell him about the procedure which I let them do. They told Dad everything that had happened when I was on the operating table.

Yasmin (Admin2)

Tuesday, 24 July, 23:01.

Doctor West

There was another business card for Doctor West in Henry's file. I typed in the website address on the card.

Doctor West's website reminded me of Mistveil's. His face was on the top of the page, he had eyes like Daniel Craig, and his degrees and qualifications were listed at the side of the page. I clicked contact and called the displayed number.

'Hello, Doctor Johnathan West's office. Bridget speaking.'

'Hi, could I speak to Doctor West please?'

'Can I ask who's calling?'

'My name is Yasmin Rivers. He doesn't know me.'

'You're not on our contact books?'

'No but-'

'Hold the line please.'

Bridget's voice was replaced by tinned Hawaiian music. She returned after a minute.

'Hello Yasmin, are you there?'

'Yeah.'

'Doctor West is busy at the moment. If you want to send him an email-'

'No. This is important. It's about Henry Andrews, the boy who died.'

She paused. Doctor West would have told his staff about Henry. Maybe they were on the lookout for phone calls like mine.

'Ok. Just one moment, please.'

She placed me back on hold and the Hawaiian music continued.

'Hello, Yasmin?' Bridget said five minutes later.

'Yeah. Hi. Can I speak to Doctor West now?'

'I'll going to transfer you through.'

'Hello, am I speaking to Yasmin Rivers?' The voice seemed to purr down the phone.

'Yeah. I'm a friend of Henry's.'

'I see. I'm Jonathan West, It's very nice to speak to you Yasmin. I imagine you have some questions for me.'

Dad sometimes spoke about disarming smiles in his business, this was the same thing but with a voice. Every question I had about Henry left my mind. I stood there, like an idiot with my mouth open, staring out of my window at a passing train.

'Yasmin, if you're comfortable with this suggestion you could come down to my office and meet me in person. You're more than welcome to bring a family member with you if you wish or a friend.'

'I'll come. On my own. Where's your office?'

Doctor West gave me his address. 'I'm free this afternoon, if you want to come? Two o'clock?'

The entrance hall in the office where Doctor West worked was amazing. Two swivel chairs hung down from the ceiling by the window which overlooked the River Thames. In the middle of the hall was a circular desk with three receptionists typing away on their computers. The walls, floor and ceiling were painted a pristine white or a pale blue, I read online that they're calming colours. The ceiling was so high it reminded me of a cathedral, the sound of heels echoed as a woman paced to the lifts behind the reception desk.

I asked one of the receptionists if I could see Doctor West. She served me a practiced smile and sent him a message on her computer. I took a seat in one of the swivel chairs and mentally prepared my questions.

How often did Henry visited you?

When did it start?

Why did he come here?

What did you talk about?

What did he say about me?

'Hello Yasmin.' His smile made me think of a grandfather looking at their favourite grandchild. His eyes were even more stunning in person.

'Hello,' I swung myself off the chair and shook his hand, the same way I had seen Dad shake hands with potential clients.

'Would you like to come up to my office?' He led me into the lift and pressed the button to the top floor. 'I was so sorry to hear of Henry's passing,' he said as the doors closed. I couldn't feel the lift moving, the only clue was a gentle hum. The place was seriously posh.

'Yeah, it sucks.'

'You were at Henry's funeral, weren't you?' he asked.

'Yeah.'

Doctor West looked at me expectantly but I didn't say anything.

The lift doors opened and we walked down a corridor decorated with motivational posters, like Mrs Saunders's office, but also pictures of sunsets and beaches.

'Did you find us okay?' Doctor West asked.

'Yeah, no problem. I live opposite Henry so I probably took the same route he took. Can I ask why you were seeing him?'

'I'm afraid I can't tell you that. Doctor patient confidentiality.'

I thought he might say that. 'Can you tell me when you heard about Henry's...' I couldn't finish the sentence.

'His mother phoned me and told me the following day. Henry was such a bright boy.'

Doctor West opened a door at the end of the corridor and led me into his office. It was literally like a Doctor's office you see in films. There's a settee that you could lay on and a chair opposite for the doctor. The window behind his desk looked out over the London skyline.

'Would you like a drink? I have tea, coffee... coke?'

He handed me a can of coke from a portable fridge behind his desk. I sat down on the edge of his settee and I winced as pain shot through my shoulder.

If Doctor West saw my pain, he didn't say anything. 'Why don't you tell me what you want to know and I'll do what I can to answer your questions?'

'Can I ask when Henry started visiting you? Like, how long did he come here for?'

'I can't give you an exact answer to that but I can say that Henry had been visiting me for a very long time.'

'Why?'

'I can't say.'

'You can't say why he came to see you?'

'No. I'm afraid that's private.'

'Did you tell him to start that blog?'

'Yes, one of our therapy ideas is that patients start online blogs or diaries to record their emotions and day to day activities. Writing is very therapeutic and Henry enjoyed making his blog. I think you can benefit from it too.'

I wondered if Doctor West had allowed me to continue writing the blog because it had helped me. It had, if I'm honest. I wanted to ask if Doctor West knew Henry's log in but that would be suspicious as fuck. Judging from Henry's first post, he made the blog alone the night he realised I was pregnant.

'Did he tell you about me?' I asked.

'I really can't say.'

'Well, he wrote about me on his blog.'

'Then you have your answer.'

'Did Henry ever say anythin'... about drugs?' I asked Doctor West.

'He wasn't on any medication that I prescribed to him.'

'But did he ever speak to you about drugs or anythin'?'

'Not to me, no.'

'It was at my house party. I didn't see who gave the drugs to him but I doubt Henry took them of his own free will.'

Doctor West nodded. 'It sounds most unlike him.'

Most unlike him? I swear, he was almost as posh as the bloody Queen.

I explained what happened that night from everyone arriving to returning from the police station. When I'd finished my story Doctor West asked me one question. 'Dean. Is your boyfriend?'

I was getting pissed off that everyone kept asking me that. 'Yeah. Well, he was. We're on and off. Did Henry tell you about him?'

'Do you mind if I ask you about him?'

'What, Dean? Why?'

Doctor West didn't answer so I asked him the first question that came to mind, 'Did you know Henry's mum and dad broke up?'

'Yes. During that time Henry made several visits to me. I helped him through the process and I must say he's making… he was making good progress.'

'So Henry was improving?' I asked.

'He was almost a completely different person if you compare him when he first started seeing me and from our last session.'

'When was that?'

'Our last session together was just before Henry did his A Levels but we spoke on the phone afterwards. The last I heard from Henry was that he was about to go to his Prom.'

The memory of Dean puking on Mrs Barton's dress seemed like a lifetime ago. It was only two weeks after my prom that I had my party.

'What advice would you normally give Henry? In, like, an normal session?'

Doctor West paused. 'I don't mind telling you because it's nothing you won't find online. I told him to participate more and to get involved. I suggested that he should spend less time on a computer screen playing games and more time enjoying life. Try new experiences. He should take more risks, albeit small ones.'

'Yeah, look where that got him.'

Doctor West nodded. I'd never seen a stranger look so sad.

'Nah, it's not your fault. Can I have another drink?'

'Of course.' Doctor West passed me another can of coke.

'You would speak to Mrs Saunders then, our school counselor?'

'Yes, we would often discuss Henry's progress. If you don't mind me asking, Yasmin, why are you so interested in Henry?'

'What'd you mean?'

'I just find it surprising,' Doctor West said, 'I would say you and Henry were complete opposites.'

'I guess he was very introverted, wasn't he, playing on his computer and Xbox all day.'

'As opposed to you?' Doctor West asked.

'Yeah. I'm always out with my friends doing somethin'.'

If Doctor West had any ideas on this, he didn't say them.

'Tell me, what do you hope to gain from this, Yasmin?'

'What do I want to gain? I want to know who gave Henry the Rose.'

'You want someone to blame?'

'No. I want to know who killed him. Who do you think killed Henry? From what I've told you, I mean?

Doctor West didn't answer my question. Instead he asked, 'Do you believe that if you can find out why Henry took the drug everything will be alright?'

'I don't like not knowing.'

Doctor West nodded. 'I understand you recently went through an abortion.'

'Yeah?'

'I don't mean to pry but as a Doctor and after everything that's happened I can't help but ask... how are you coping?'

I almost laughed. 'I had my debriefing session earlier this week. I'm fine with what happened. I'm just not fine with what happened to Henry.'

I wiped away a tear hoping Doctor West wouldn't notice but he had. Before I could stop myself I was bawling.

When I left the clinic a couple of hours later I felt better. Lighter. I could see why Henry liked talking things to him. Like Henry said in his first post, it's good to unpack everything.

Yasmin (Admin2)

Wednesday, 25 July, 11:38.

Passwords

I sent out another message today but out of the fifty people I sent the first message too, twenty have blocked me. Still no answer from the remaining. I was so pissed off that I wanted to go round their houses and physically ask them but I didn't know where most of them lived.

I've made a few more guesses on Henry's password.

The Average. Theaverage. Theaverage01. Yasminissexyaf.

I've reread Henry's post about me hacking into Mrs Barton's account during his detention but this is different.

The problem is that people are moving away to uni soon. Chelsea posted a picture of what her room is meant to look like in her halls and that's what really shook me. People having been making Facebook status about confirming their place in dorms the like and that's when I realised how little time I have left.

Yasmin (Admin2)

Wednesday, 25 July, 21:13.

Clara

Dad has always liked my older sister, Clara, more than me. She was easier to control, I was a wild child. Clara is at uni in Hull studying mechanics. She's jarring when she's at home but I miss her anyway. Dad spends most of his free time phoning, skyping or visiting her.

I was in the kitchen when I heard Dad's Ipad ringing. It was Clara with a FaceTime call.

'Hey,' I heard Clara say when I pressed accept. It took a second for the video to come up.

'Hi, sis.'

'Oh, hi Yas.'

'How's Uni?'

'Yeah... yeah it's alright. Dad around? I've got a question about bills.'

'He's in his office. You sound a bit husky.'

'Fuck, never mind. Yeah, I've got a cold. What was that thing you commented on, on Facebook the other day? Some boy dying?'

'Henry. He was my friend.'

I told Clara what had happened and when I'd finished you could tell she was thinking of something thoughtful to say.

'Well that fucking sucks.'

Dad found us chatting in the front room an hour later. I listened to her conversation with Dad from the top of the stairs. She told him what she had told me, she had a new boyfriend and had a new job as a waitress in Byron's. He helped her with the bills and then shouted at her off for not taking tablets for her cold.

Yasmin (Admin2)

Friday, 27 July, 22:18.

Support group

I had a phone call yesterday from a woman called Helen. She explained that she was the leader of the support group and that she had spoken to Sergeant Terrell and Mrs Saunders about me.

'I really think we can help you here, Yasmin,' she kept saying. It was like when one of those call centres phone you and you can't put the phone down on them because you feel like a terrible person. I promised her I would go, mostly to get her off the phone and then Dad promised he would drive me there and pick me up afterwards.

It was depressing. I'm not saying support groups are useless because I know people benefit from them but it didn't help me at all. It made everything seem worse. The group sat in a circle and spoke in either depressed voices or in a forced cheerfulness. Helen went around the group doing introductions. The repetition of mentioning the dead and how great they were, over and over, made me feel like crying. Christ.

'Yasmin, would you like to introduce yourself?' Helen asked when she reached me.

'Oh... okay. Hi, I'm Yasmin Rivers, I'm eighteen. My friend, best friend I guess, died. He OD'ed.'

'Yasmin, I'm sorry to hear that,' Helen said. She had that phrase so many times during the session that it'd lost all meaning. It was like she had these default lines saved inside her brain. 'Why don't you tell us more about him?'

But I didn't want to. Henry was a great guy and sharing my friendship with him felt like revealing a secret. I shook my head and sat down.

At the end of the meeting Helen and a few others came over to me and invited me to their next session. They gave me tons of leaflets and tried to pry deeper into my friendship with Henry.

'How old was he, dear?' a woman asked, 'I lost my first husband when I was twenty seven.'

'I battled drugs for most of my life,' said a balding man with no teeth. 'I know how dangerous they are.'

'We're here every other Friday,' Helen said gesturing around the church hall. I dodged their questions, made vague promises, found Dad in the car park and went home.

Yasmin (Admin2)

Sunday, 29 July, 24:12.
Evelyn Petunia Rivers

Something interesting happened when I watching TV with Dad this evening. We watched *24 Hours in A&E* where a tree surgeon fell out of a tree and was cut by his own chainsaw. Then we watched *Who Do You Think You Are?* It's a show where historian's research a celebrity's family history and discover one of their relatives was either really famous, died in a war somewhere or had a really cool historical job. I wasn't really watching to be honest. I was re-reading Henry's blog on my phone when one of the historians on TV showed the celebrity his great grandmother's birth certificate.

Dolores Petunia Cainwright.

'That's your mum's middle name, Petunia,' Dad said. I looked up as Dad never really talked about Mum since she died. 'Evelyn Petunia Rivers.'

'That's a nice name,' I said.

Yasmin (Admin2)

Wednesday, 1 August, 22:27.
Starting sessions with Doctor West

I was finishing *Gossip Girl* last night when my phone rang. I thought it could be the police or maybe a shop I'd dropped my CV into.

'Hello Yasmin? It's Doctor West.'

'Doctor West, h-how are you?'

'I'm fine, thanks for asking. I called to ask how you are, actually.'

'Me? I'm...' I was going to say fine but that wasn't true. 'I'm okay.'

Fuck. I read somewhere that if you say that to a Doctor they think it's a secret SOS. Doctor West seemed to pick up on it.

'I know you're not my patient Yasmin but seeing as you are a friend of Henry's, I thought you might benefit from some theory sessions with me. How does that sound?'

It sounded brilliant. Doctor West spoke about Henry in the present tense which made me like him even more.

'What about Mrs Saunders?' I asked. 'Won't you have to tell her?'

'No. Henry was recommended to me by Mrs Saunders. Since she has nothing to do with your joining, she won't need to know.'

'What about the cost? I'm sorry, I don't think my Dad can afford-'

'There's no charge. This is a favour.'

'Okay... When do you want me to see you?'

'I'm free tomorrow afternoon at four?'

Doctor West met me in reception again and took me up to his office. After he had given me a drink and told me to sit down on the settee, the questions began. 'How are things at home with your family?'

I explained that Mum wasn't around anymore and that I lived with my Dad. Then I burst out crying. I was surprised because normally when you cry you can feel you are about to cry but this was sudden.

Mum died when I was four. I don't remember much of it because I was so young. Mum had been given medicine from the doctors to treat a chest infection but she'd had an allergic reaction to the tablets and died when Dad, Clara and I were out shopping. We came home, I was carrying shopping bags of frozen food from Asda and we found her there, facing the TV, the light of the screen bathing her body. Since then Dad became a hypochondriac, he's scared of getting ill. It's why Clara didn't want to take her medicine for her cold and why I refused to take tablets for the operation.

'Does your Dad know about your abortion?' Doctor West asked me.

'Yeah. I t-told him the other week.'

'How did he take it?'

'We were having a row and it sort of... came out,' I stuttered. 'What about Henry's mum though? She's lost her husband and now she's lost Henry. Do you think sh-she'll be okay?'

Doctor West assured me that Henry's mum would be okay. I wondered if she was having sessions with Doctor West, like I was. Maybe Mrs Barton was too. That might be why she had Doctor West's card on her desk. We spent most of the two hour period talking about me, what I liked and disliked, what my plans were for the future and stuff like that.

'I pick up my results tomorrow,' I said at the end of the session. I'd been thinking about it on the train there and it was terrifying me.

'How do you think you did?'

'Shit.'

'Well, we'll have to wait and see won't we?'

Yasmin (Admin2)

Thursday, 2 August, 23:19.
Results day

I don't like the idea of exams and I'm not just saying that because I'm a bad student. Imagine, you've been revising all year for your exams, you've gone to every revision session, completed every bit of coursework and you're ready for your exam. Then your grandparent dies or your bus to school is cancelled. Tough shit. Also the stress exams put students under is fucking ridiculous. I've known people to have mental breakdowns under the pressure. Adults keep telling us that the exams are the most important things in our lives and they're only partly right. Our A Levels and GCSE's are the most important things in our lives so far. Worse is yet to come.

There was a crowd of former Sixth formers in the school carpark, waiting outside the fire door to the school hall but no one there I could call a friend. I texted Megan on the train home yesterday, asking what time she wanted to pick up her results but she said she was going to pick them up alone at the end of the day. I saw Chelsea at the back crowd but she was deliberately not looking in my direction. Adam and Joe were chatting by the fire door but I thought I should stay clear of them. I stood there, at the school gate, like a loner staring at my phone until Mrs Barton opened the fire doors and everyone shoved their way inside.

I ran for the nearest results table. My maths teacher didn't look at me, she just held out an envelope.

'Thanks,' I said but she was already speaking to one of her favourite students about their high grade. I ripped open the envelope.

Maths: D

Whatever.

I pushed through the crowd and snatched up an envelope bearing my name on the Spanish results table. The only reason I chose Spanish is because Spanish men are hot but I regretted taking the class since the first lesson.

Spanish: E

It took me several minutes to reach the sports studies table and convince the teacher to give me my result. I extracted myself from the throng of people and ripped open the envelope.

Sport studies: D

'How are you getting on?'

Mrs Barton had appeared behind me.

'Er... okay so far.' I held my results at my side, turning them away so she couldn't see my grades.

'Good. I... hope you do well.' Mrs Barton looked awkward and I felt a bit sorry for her, to be honest.

'Thanks, I'm sure I'll be okay.'

I spotted Mr Roth at a table on the far side of the hall.

'I need to get my geography result, can I...'

Mrs Barton nodded and I sprinted to the geography table.

'Do you have mine?' I asked Mr Roth.

He looked around and then offered me the envelope, the same way a drug dealer would look around before selling drugs in a shitty TV show.

'Do you know what it is?' I asked as I opened the envelope.

'Yeah, we were are given a spreadsheet with everyone's results on them yesterday.'

'Do you know Henry's grades?' I asked.

Mr Roth nodded as took out my piece of paper with my grade.

Geography: B

Mr Roth grinned. 'Your coursework was very impressive,' he said. 'You clearly put a lot of effort in.'

I didn't tell him it was me and Henry. 'I need to phone my dad and tell him.'

I rushed back to the school carpark, to phone Dad. The local media were there talking to the high achievers about their A grades, Adam was upset because he only scored a B and not an A in one of his subjects. The teachers either look proud or smug depending on which student they were talking to.

Grace approached me holding her results. 'What did you get?' she asked.

'Enough to get into college.' I lied.

'Congrats.' Then she hugged me. 'I'm so sorry,' she whispered into my ear.

'It's fine, I'm sorry too.'

There was a roar from the other side of the carpark. Dean revved into sight wearing his leathers and his helmet, visor lowered. He dismounted his bike and marched through the fire door, shoving Joe aside as he emerged.

I realised that Henry was right, this was going to be the last time I'd see most of these people.

And I want them to remember me.

I waited till Dean was inside before taking out my house keys and scraping them along the bodywork of the bike.

The sound was beautiful.

Then I had another idea. I wanted Dean to stick around and be humiliated, like he's been humiliating Henry and his friends all year. I unscrewed the air caps on his bike's tyres.

A few of the kids started to cheer. By the time I'd reached the last tyre I had attracted a crowd.

'He's coming,' Grace shouted.

The crowd scattered. I reached the pavement and pretended to text as Dean came out of the school, clutching his unopened results.

'No. Fuck no. My bike, man. What the fuck? Who did this shit? Who?'

Nobody answered Dean, they just laughed. I smirked and pocketed my phone. When I looked up Henry's mum was standing watching me from the opposite pavement.

She gave me a weak smile, 'I saw all that.'

'Oh.'

'Did you get your results?' she asked.

'Yeah.'

'What'd you get?' She crossed the street. I didn't know if I should run or not.

'I got a B in geography.'

'How wonderful. Your dad must be so proud.'

There a pause where both of us didn't know what to say.

'Did you pick up Henry's…'

'Yeah, I got 'em here,' she held up four unsealed envelopes.

'What did he get?' I asked but I know at once it was the wrong thing to say.

She started to cry. 'He-he could have gone to college if he wanted to.'

I hugged her and felt her body shudder against mine as we stood there.

'C'mon,' I said after a minute or two, 'let's get something to eat, eh?'

I walked with Henry's mum to a greasy spoon café on the high street. Carol ordered a jacket potato, I ordered a steak and kidney pie. Carol was still sobbing.

'What results did you get? she asked me as the waitress returned to the counter. I don't think I've ever had a proper conversation with Henry's mum, I spoke to her briefly when I was in primary school but that was it. Now I could see how similar she and Henry looked.

'Two D's, one E and one B.'

'How many UCAS points is that?'

'Fuck knows.' I said. I shrugged out of my hoodie.

Carol laughed and used a napkin to wipe her tears. 'What's your plan now?' she asked me.

'I can apply for an art college if I want to or a beauty course maybe. I might retake Sixth form to get more points. I dunno yet, I'm going to talk to Dad about it when I get home.'

'Henry had enough points to go to a college to do an English course but I don't think he was really into it,' Carol said, 'I could just tell, you know?'

She's right, Henry said that he wanted to drop out during the first term. I wondered if Carol knew about the blog or the fact Henry helped me with my operation. I was going to ask what grades Henry got but it doesn't really matter.

We made small talk until the waitress delivered our food. Carol's potato was soggy and my pie crumbled when I poked it with the fork but I didn't complain.

'I'm sorry.' I'd meant to tell Carol about the party but those words came out instead.

'I know.'

'I really am though. I'm so sorry.'

'I know. It's not your fault.'

I told her what I remembered of Henry at the party.

'How's your dad taking it?' Carol asked.

I was actually surprised she was asking about Dad. 'Oh, he's fine. He's just come back from Scotland visiting my sister.'

'I thought she lived in Hull now?'

'She does. She was hiking in Scotland and Dad met her up there.'

'I can remember her when she was still at primary school,' Carol trailed off. 'I'm sorry about attacking you. In Sainsbury's, I mean. It was… the first time I left the house since-'

'Oh.' I mentally counted how long had passed between my party and Carol's attack. A month and a bit maybe? I would have gone crazy.

'I had eighty six condolences cards and twelve bouquets of flowers in the end,' Carol said.

I couldn't stop thinking about what is must have been like when the police told her Henry had died. 'I was at the funeral.'

'Yes, I saw you at the back with Henry's teacher. It was a good turnout.'

'The day before,' I said, 'there was something going on in your back garden.'

'Yes, I had the family stay over. It was our own private funeral. Henry's uncle, Patrick is staying with me. He stayed for a couple of nights when Paul left. He'll look after me.'

I didn't realise that Henry had such a big family. 'How's Wilfred?' I asked not knowing what else to say.

'He's fine. Well, no he's whining and keeps sitting by the f-front door.'

'And Henry's dad?'

'Paul's buggered off with his boss from work. Now the divorce papers are being processed, he's moving out to Spain with that Linda woman. Paul spent time with Henry before his exams and I think Henry was thankful for that. I still talk to Paul but… y'know?'

'It's difficult.'

'Yeah, I'm moving out too I think,' Carol said. 'Nothing for me here now, is there?'

I just nodded and sipped my drink. It's my fault she's moving out. If I didn't fuck up Henry would be here.

When I got home I told Dad my results and he was so happy that he gave me a hug. As he rang Clara to tell her I looked on Facebook to see what everyone else had scored.

Adam got his A in drama, two B's and a C. He's going to Uni.

Joe had one B and three C's. He's going to college.

Chelsea had someone film her opening her results. Three C's.

She's got into Uni.

Megan hasn't made a status with her results but I saw her in the background of Chelsea's video, proving she lied to me. She must of got piss poor grades, like me. Chelsea was always the smart one.

Dean hasn't made a status either.

I'm not going to put my results up. I'm happy with them but compared to everyone else's they're shit.

Yasmin (Admin2)

Friday, 3 August, 18:43.

Henry's Dad

Carol told me Henry's dad's new address but when I visited his house the letterbox was stuffed with leaflets, meaning he hadn't been there for several days. Then I went to McDonald's ordered a drink and a Big Mac and stalked Paul's Facebook page. He'd turned on his privacy setting, I couldn't see anything other than his profile picture of himself and Linda. Linda was tagged in the picture so I clicked the link back to her profile.

Linda Roberts.

Studied Business at Birmingham University

Lives in London

In a relationship with Paul Andrews.

I browsed through her pictures. I didn't get a good look at her during the funeral, she's in her late thirties, brown hair, green eyes, a coy smile. Her profile picture is of her on a dance floor, holding a cocktail glass. She's a lot slimmer than Carol.

Then I started looking through her wall. The most recent update was twelve hours ago.

Linda Roberts checked into The Sunset Hotel at King's Cross with Paul Andrews. Can't wait to get away to the sun.

It took me an hour and a half to reach the hotel, it was a few streets away King's Cross station. I asked the receptionist what room Linda Roberts was in and when she looked doubtful I said I needed her because there was a family emergency.

I knocked twice on the door.

'Who is it?' A male voice asked.

'I'm looking for Mr Andrews.'

A pause. 'What'd you want?'

'I need to talk to you about Henry.'

I heard hushed whispers from inside.

'If you don't come out now I'll tell your wife where you are,' I shouted.

There was a thump and the sound of the bolt across the door being withdrawn. Out stepped Henry's dad wearing nothing but Y fronts.

'Jesus, Yasmin, what you doin' here?' He pulled the door too.

'I'm on my own,' I said as he glanced down the corridor. 'I want to talk about Henry.'

I caught a glimpse of the hotel room behind him. Clothes on the floor, the curtains were drawn and it reeked of BO. There was movement from within the bed, Linda wrapped her body within the sheets and peeked out at me, like a frightened kitten.

Henry's dad stared at me and honest to God I thought he was going to hit me.

'Wait here,' he said and slammed the door in my face before I could answer.

Paul remerged from the room five minutes later, dressed but he hadn't put on any deodorant. He took me to the hotel's cafe and ordered himself a bacon sandwich.

'What do you want, then?' Paul asked.

'I want to tell you what happened.'

'I saw you at the funeral,' he said between mouthfuls of his bacon butty. 'I didn't think you would come.'

'I was close with Henry.'

'I know, that's why I'm surprised you came. I thought it'll be too much for you.'

I didn't answer that. I had chosen to wear my hoodie but everyone else was dressed really posh. I could sense them staring at me, like everyone had stared at me when I had first gone to Summer School.

'I'm sorry about Henry,' I said.

'Ain't your fault,' Paul lied. 'What happened at your party, Yasmin?'

To be honest, I was getting pretty pissed off with everyone asking me that. Henry's dad was annoying too, he wouldn't look at me in the eye. He wasn't angry, I could tell from his body language, he was tired. It took me an hour to tell him what happened because he kept interrupting me with stupid questions.

'Henry should have known better,' Paul said when I'd finished, 'but he was under a lot of pressure.'

'When we met last time he said how he was helping you with something big. Before I left he was talking about how much time he was spending at your house.'

Christ, the last time they spoke was on the day of the operation.

'What was he helping you with?' Paul asked.

'A school project, nothing serious,' I said, 'my geography coursework.'

Henry's dad finished his sandwich. 'How's Carol?'

I only just realised that the café had the radio on and they were playing that fucking song again, "Cold Embrace."

'Okay,' I said, 'she's getting a lot of family support. She said her brother is living with her now.'

'Good, she'll hate be alone. Did she tell you I'm moving out to Spain with Linda?'

'Yeah, losing your son and then your husband.'

He glowered at me. 'When you're older you'll understand.'

'Understand what?'

'Why relationships end when they do.'

I thought that was a fucking cheek.

Yasmin (Admin2)

Saturday, 4 August, 22:57.

Normal life

I don't know who killed Henry. I've spoken to Doctor West and we've agreed on what we think the most likely solution is. Henry took the Rose because he wanted to impress everyone but mostly me. He wanted to be cool and not feel left out. There is a chance that someone gave Henry the Rose but even if that were true I couldn't prove anything.

I've still not had luck with Henry's password. After reading every entry and discussing him with everyone I still don't know how Henry's mind worked, I can't second guess his password.

Doctor West said that I should keep the blog going if I wanted to but he said he wanted me to carry on with my life. I'm to report back to him next week.

Yasmin (Admin2)

Monday, 6 August, 20:51.

Sainsbury's Job interview

I had an interview at Sainsbury's today. They had a job fair where you can go and meet the employers and see what they are looking for in their staff.

When I arrived I realised I was under dressed. Everyone was wearing suits or smart/casual clothes. I was wearing ripped jeans, a T shirt and my hoodie. I followed the group of people into an office and the Manager of the store gave a talk about how delighted she was to see us and what a brilliant opportunity it was for us. It reminded me of a school assembly. She kept rambling for an hour. Then we were lead into a staff room to socialise and one by one we were called back into the office to be interviewed by the Manager. I was fed up of waiting and was about to leave when she called me in.

I can't remember the Manager's name but when I walked in she gave me one of those great big fake smiles.

'Hello there,' she leant across the table to shake my hand. 'What's your name?'

'Yasmin.' I hate interviews. I don't like the way people look at me.

'Yasmin, lovely to meet you. Tell me, which role are you most interested in?'

'I was thinking of working on the tills.'

'Ah, okay. Customer service then. Do you have a copy of your CV I can look at?'

I took my CV out of my pocket, unfolded it and passed it across the table. I saw her smile falter as she realised it was only half a page long.

'Thank you. I'll make sure you're put under consideration. Are there any questions you'd like to ask me about the role?'

'Er...No. No, I'm good thanks.'

The Manager stood up and shook my hand again. 'Yasmin, it's been lovely meeting you. Take care.'

She flashed me another killer smile as I left.

When I returned home Dad asked me how it went. I told him it was fine. Then I stopped and told him the truth, that it was a waste of time and there was no way I was going to get the job.

Dad said he couldn't see me working in a shop, neither can I, but he was glad I had applied.

Yasmin (Admin2)

Wednesday, 8 August, 10:31.

Learning to drive

I've never driven before. I've never really thought about it, Dean used to take me everywhere on the back of his bike. Now I don't speak to him and I need my own car. And I can't buy one if I don't know how to drive it.

Grace past her driving test the other day and left her driving instructor's details on Facebook. Her instructor's name is Margaret Underhill. I've booked a lesson next Friday.

Yasmin (Admin2)

Saturday, 11 August, 13:48

Sessions

Doctor West said today was my final free session but promised me a discount if I wanted to book myself with him in the future.

'How'd you think you're doing Yasmin?' He asked me.

'Alright.'

'Do you think you're improving?'

'I guess. I don't cry anymore. I just… do.'

'Would you like to expand on that?'

'I just do what you suggested. Try to carry on my normal life, y'know?'

'And how do you feel about normal life, about moving on?'

'I'm okay.'

'Are you happy?'

I just shrugged.

Yasmin (Admin2)

Friday, 17 August, 17:23.

Driving in a thunderstorm

My first driving lesson was in a thunderstorm. I ran from the front door to the instructor's car and clambered inside, soaked.

'Nice to meet you, Yasmin.' Margaret said offering her hand, 'shame about the weather, isn't it?' She looked like Granny from the Looney Tunes cartoons. As I clasped her hand there was a smack caused by the rain water. I wiped my hand on the seat as Margaret pulled away from the kerb with a grimace.

'I've been driving since I was twenty, and teaching people like yourself how to drive since I was forty,' she said. I made the correct noises at the right moment to pretend I was listening. My clothes were sticking to my skin, my phone was digging into my leg and I was too scared to listen properly.

'I've never once had an accident. Have you had any driving experience before?' she asked.

'What? No, no. Well yeah, once.'

'Once?'

'My ex-boyfriend let me drive his quad bike once.' It was actually completely illegal but you say things like that without thinking, don't you?

'I think you'll find driving a car is much different to driving a quad bike, Mrs Rivers.' She called me Mrs Rivers, not a word of a lie.

Margaret turned into Hillberry Road and taught me about the pedals and gears.

We swapped seats when the rain eased off and she asked me to start the car. 'Put the keys in the ignition and turn them clockwise,' she instructed.

I twisted the keys. The electronics of the car turned on.

'Foot on the clutch and twist the key.'

'I know, I know, I got this.'

My shoe, wet with rain, slipped on the peddles and the car jerked.

'Oh dear. Try again.'

It took me three attempts before I had the engine running.

We spent the rest of the lesson driving up and down the road, going from first to second gear and back again. Margaret said I kept driving in the middle of the road but that this was normal for first time drivers.

As Margaret drove me home she talked about her past students. You'd think she taught Lewis Hamilton how to drive or something. I booked a time and date for my next session and sprinted through the rain to the front door.

'How was it?' Dad asked when I came inside.

I spent the next ten minutes explaining the little I had done and nodded when Dad gave me the same advice Margate had given me. After dinner he made me practice turning a steering wheel by using a dinner plate.

Yasmin (Admin2)

Sunday, 2 September, 09:20

Blocked

Out of the fifty people I've messaged about Henry, thirty nine have blocked me.

None of them have answered my messages.

Yasmin (Admin2)

Tuesday, 17 September, 16:45.

Everyone's leaving

The only one of my friends to go to University is Chelsea. She's going to Stanlow to do a psychology degree which is weird because I thought she hated her psychology classes.

I phoned her this afternoon. 'Are you actually leaving for Uni?' I asked her.

'Yeah.'

'A psychology course?'

'Yeah.'

'I thought you hated psychology, though?'

'I do,' she said, 'but it's what I'm good at. I've got to do something, haven't I?'

'Well, we need to celebrate.'

'Can't.'

'Why the hell not? We could-' I was going to say get drinks but I stopped myself.

'Because I'm leaving tomorrow. I'm spending this evening with my family. Look, sorry I got to go.' She hung up on me.

Megan is retaking two of her exams so she's going back to Sixth form next year. Dean has a job working with his dad on a builder's site which is what he always said he was going to do. His dad promised him a place. Maybe that's unfair but what are you going to do? I haven't spoken to Jake recently but Megan told me on the first day of Summer School that he'd going into his second year at his art college.

I watched everyone leave on Facebook. It wasn't an official event it was a continuous stream on my newsfeed. Everyone posted a status, there were selfies inside cars packed with luggage, family pictures, shared baby photos. In the end I turned my phone off and watched *Mean Girls*.

Yasmin (Admin2)

Tuesday, 17 September, 17:32.

Joe

Dad sent me round the shop to buy milk. As I approached the zebra crossing a car stopped to let me pass. I had my Ipod in but as I was crossing I glanced into the car. Joe was driving and the back seat was stacked with suitcases. He gave me a nod as I crossed and drove away.

I don't know if Joe will forgive me, I don't know if he should to be honest but I hope he does well at college.

Yasmin (Admin2)

Wednesday, 18 September, 19:11

What I'm going to do?

I spoke to Dad about what I'm going to do now Sixth form is over. I don't want to do a course at college I wouldn't like. I can't get a job and I don't have the grades to go to university even though Henry was right when he said I would enjoy that life.

Dad and I agreed that the best thing I could do was to go into year fourteen and get more UCAS points. Then I can join a course at a decent college next year. Me and Dad had a meeting with Mrs Barton this morning. She smiled a lot and didn't act like a bitch. She said it wouldn't be as bad next year because I would have her full support and the year group, although they had heard of Henry, didn't know him and wouldn't know me. I start on Monday.

Yasmin (Admin2)

Thursday, 19 September, 19:01.

Second driving lesson

Dad brought me all these driving books which I've put in my room and ignored. He's already talking about my theory test. For my second lesson Margaret took me back to Hillberry Road and I drove up and down it at low speed. It was fine for the first hour but then a coach arrived. Turns out we kept driving past a retirement home and the OAP's were returning from a day trip to Brighton. Driving past the coach was a bloody nightmare. I can't express how stressed I was in that moment. The coach blocked half the road, the old people kept tutting at me and staring through the coach window, I stalled the car three times and Margaret was talking nonstop throughout about how bad I was.

When it was finally over I asked if we could end the lesson early so I could go home. Margaret gave me a look as though I was a piece of shit she had stepped in and said, 'I think that's a good idea.'

Yasmin (Admin2)

Friday, 20 September, 16:46.
Gardening

I've spent the morning deep cleaning the house with Dad. The last time we deep cleaned was when Dad returned from Scotland after the party. Normally Dad is on top of this sort of thing but with everything going on he's let it slip.

We spent the morning cleaning inside while listening to the radio and in the afternoon we worked outside in the sun. We cut down the ivy that had been climbing up the wall and then we cleaned the roof gutter. It was disgusting because the gutter was filled with rotting leaves and rainwater. We laughed and chatted throughout the day and when we'd finished and had a shower Dad ordered pizza for dinner. It was nice not to be shouting at each another.

Yasmin (Admin2)

Friday, 20 September, 22:38.
My final driving lesson

The plan was to pull out from the junction by the library and to go down the high street before taking the next turning off. We arrived at the T junction and waited. Turns out that there was a lorry on its side on the motorway and the traffic had been directed through Norcrest High Street. I was waiting at the junction for ten minutes but no one stopped to let me out. Then I realised that it was this junction where I was knocked off my bike chasing Henry's funeral. That really pissed me off because if Henry had continued taking his lessons he would have passed his test by now. I tried pulling forwards, edging my way out but Margaret stopped me by stamping on the brakes.

'Not until it's clear, not until it's clear,' she kept saying. A lorry had seen us and stopped but the car had stalled. The lorry driver blasted his horn which bloody near deafened me and I fumbled with the keys.

Margaret jabbered on but I couldn't hear her. I was too hot in my hoodie, the traffic behind the lorry was sounding their horns and the noise mixed into one continuous roar.

I snatched the keys out the ignition, rammed them back in and twisted. The engine spluttered.

People were starting to stare from the pavement, the traffic on the other side of the road were slowing down to watch.

It took me five attempts to get the engine going again. Then Margaret took a hold of the steering wheel and drove us down the high street to the next turning. As we turned off the lorry driver shouting something and flicked us his middle finger.

'I have never seen such dangerous behaviour-' Margaret started to screech but then she saw I was crying, I swear the pitying look on her face made me want to punch her.

It wasn't my fault, was it? Everything was has happening too fast. There was too much noise too think and honestly I don't even need to learn to drive. Where would I drive too? How could I afford to buy a car?

Margaret drove me home and said that when I was ready I should book another lesson.

I won't.

Yasmin (Admin2)

Saturday, 21 September, 02:23.

The Worst thing

I was walking back from the shops yesterday and a car drove past me, its windows down and the radio blaring.

"When I wished you were mine, I wish I was told, you were a criminal, the best in the world."

I hate that fucking song.

I just can't continue like everything is bloody normal. I hate not knowing, that's the worst thing.

When you read this Doctor West, please call me.

Yasmin (Admin2)

Saturday, 21 September, 13:51.

Dean

I phoned the number Sergeant Rickman had left me and gave the case reference number to the officer on the phone. He told me there were no updates because the case had been closed. He then started telling me how to appeal to have the case reopened but he sounded so bored, like I was the hundredth caller to ask him that, so I hung up.

Everyone has left. Then I smoked my first cigarette in two months. The first drag felt great but then I felt so shit about it that I dropped the rest of the cig out the window and logged back into Facebook. I scrolled through everyone's Facebook wall who was at the party. It was hard because some of them had multiple accounts and many were inactive or had blocked to me. I started two hours ago. I ended up on Jake's Facebook and scrolled down, past the date of the party until I found a comment by Dean on Jake's wall. They were talking about a rave they had been planning to go to, two months before my party.

I'm ready to get wrecked, boi. You going to bring Rosie tomorrow?

Yasmin (Admin2)

Saturday, 21 September, 17:54.
What Dean had to say

I texted Dean and told him I was alone so he would come over.

Me: Hey, what you up to?

Dean: Nothing much, Y?

Me: I'm all by myself this evening..

Dean: Want me to come over? Lol

Me: Yeah. XX

Dean's taken the baffler out of his bike, so I heard him coming. His dad probably gave him the money to repair his bike. His daddy buys him whatever he wants and if he doesn't Dean throws a temper tantrum.

'Hey,' I said.

'Hey baby,' he leaned in for a kiss but I pulled back. 'No one else in?' he asked, looking into the house.

'Dad's up in London for a contract. He won't be back till late.' I hadn't told Dad about my plan because he'd just try to stop me.

'Cool.' Dean strolled inside and went upstairs leaving me to shut the front door.

When I reached my bedroom, Dean had taken his hoodie and shirt off. I was going to ask him about last night and try to extract an answer out of him but he was laying on the bed in the same position that he was the night of the party. I completely lost my shit.

'What the fuck?'

The fact that Dean looked genuinely confused really pissed me off. 'What the fuck are you doing?'

'You called me over,' he whined.

'Not for that, put your fuckin' shirt back on. I wanna talk. Listen. Henry-'

'Jesus Christ.'

'He's fucking dead, Dean. Don't roll your eyes at-'

'I know he's dead! I watched the coffin go past the school. Listen, yeah? Henry was a good kid, alright? I know you were friends,' he said friends as though it was an insult, 'but you have to let go, yeah? He's dead. He's fuckin' dead and nothin' is going to bring him back.'

'I know that,' I screamed. My voice cracked. 'He died under my roof. He died in my front room.'

'Fuck.' Dean stomped to my window. 'Shit happens, Yas. People die all the time, all over the world.' I could see Henry's bedroom behind him.

'Henry didn't deserve to die,' I tried to say but I sort of sobbed it instead.

'So what? The good people die just as much as the bad.'

'But Henry had… he could have been somethin.'

'Pah.'

'He didn't get U's and E's like you, dickhead. He didn't flunk out like me. Someone gave him a drug. Someone could have killed him. Do you know who?'

'You know I don't know.' He punched his waxed chest. The only reason he waxed it was because he thought it looked sexy but I think he's been watching too much porn.

'You sound like the fuckin' police. Do you know how many times they came to my house after it happened? Do you?'

'Do you know who OD'ed him,' I asked again.

'Why do you… why do you think someone gave him the drug? Henry could have taken some for himself.'

'Henry would never take it. We both know that. Not of his own will. He just wouldn't.'

'Oh, and you would know that, wouldn't you? How long have you been fucking him, Yas?'

'I've not-'

Dean's cheeks flapped up and down like a bulldog's. Normally I'd find that funny but his spit was landing on my face and he was so close I could feel his breath. 'Bullshit. Bull, fucking, shit. He loved you, everyone knew that. He was fuckin' obsessed.'

'Henry-'

'Was a lonely little virgin pining after you for most of the fuckin' year.'

'No, He was just a good kid. I-'

'So you fucking admit it then? Eh? You slept with him?'

'No. I never-'

Dean placed his hands on my shoulders and screamed in my face. 'Did you fuck him?'

I thought he was going to hit me. I tried to push him away but I couldn't break his grip.

'Let go of me.'

Dean hesitated and then softened his grip. 'Yas, a boy like Henry ain't good for you. You need someone that can actually...'

'Someone like you? Piss off.'

He punched my desk. My CV's fluttered onto the floor.

'I was pregnant.' I blurted it out, just like that.

'You...you what?' His anger evaporated, like someone had pulled the plug in a sink and his emotions had just drained away.

'I was... pregnant. I took a test and I'd been pregnant for a couple of months. But I had an abortion.'

Dean eyes scanned my stomach.

'It was your baby, Dean. Do you understand that, yeah? I had an abortion, on your baby.'

'What?' Dean said again. 'Pregnant?'

'Yeah. Henry knew. I told him and he was helping me through it.'

Dean sat down on the edge of my bed. 'You were pregnant,' he said again as though he didn't know what that meant.

'Henry helped me with the abortion. Henry helped me with my school stuff.'

'Why?'

'What?'

'Why though? It was my kid, weren't it? We could have named it and...'

I thought he was going to be sick. 'Because you weren't around. You bloody fucked off with that Elle girl didn't you or you were mucking around on your bike.'

'Did you... kill it?' he asked.

I don't know how to answer that question. I don't regret what I did.

'It wasn't even alive, though.'

I didn't say anything else. Part of me wanted to go and put my hand on his shoulder, or give him a hug and ask if he was alright, but if I did that, I knew he'd lash out. Another part of me wanted to talk about Henry, but I couldn't bring myself to say it. 'I'd kill Henry,' Dean said. 'He… I…'

I'd kill Henry. He'd kill Henry if he could. Meaning he didn't before.

'Did you bring drugs to the party, Dean?' I said but Dean wasn't listening.

'I need to go,' he said, 'before it gets dark out.'

'De-'

But he was gone. By the time I reached the the front door Dean was racing away on his bike.

Yasmin (Admin2)

Saturday, 30 June, 03:12.
Yasmin's Party (Draft)

I'm at Yasmin's party and everyone seems to be enjoying themselves. There's a DJ stand in the front room and people are dancing. Yasmin emptied her dad's drinks cupboard, everyone is drunk. She's upstairs with Dean. I don't know why he's here but Yasmin seems okay with him now. Apart from Yasmin and Dean there are a few other people here I know like Megan and Chelsea but they're not my friends so I can't really talk to them. There are about fifty people here in total. A group were just talking about *Lord of the Rings* but they didn't really understand the films and when I explained what the Balrog was they just stared at me. Jake overheard me and did this smoke trick with the speakers. He's blew smoke from his mouth in a perfect ring then we watched it shatter against the speaker. Just like Gandalf. Dean told him to give me a cigarette but it was a different brand to what Yasmin smokes. I didn't like it.

Doctor West said I should socialise more but I find that difficult with strangers. Sometimes I find it hard to socialise with Adam and Joe. Mum said that conversations happen naturally but they don't when I'm around.

I'm not normally a party person but everyone here seems to be having fun.

Henry (Admin1)

Sunday, 22 September, 12:02.

What happened to Henry

I knew there was going to be drugs at my party. I knew Henry wouldn't take any of them and I knew he wouldn't grass us up. When Henry arrived and realised he didn't know anyone he started working on his blog on his phone because he didn't know what else to do. Dean saw this and he was still pissed off with Henry from prom and he was jealous of how close Henry was to me. He told Jake to give Henry a Rose. He wanted to see Henry fucked up but he didn't want to kill him. Jake was way too high to realise how powerful he had made the Rose and everyone was too pissed and high to see Henry OD behind Jake's DJ stand. There were drugs on Jake's DJ equipment which was why he'd been asking about it.

I went to Henry's house and told his mum. I explained about my abortion, how supportive Henry was with it, what happened at the party and what I'd been doing since. I showed her Henry's blog on her Ipad because I think she has the right to know. I sat with her in the front room, with Wilfred on her lap and we read through every post Henry has written and then my own.

Then I showed her Henry's final post, I published it before I left my house. Dean mentioned naming our child and that got me thinking about child names and I remembered Henry's suggestion. Henry's password was Charis. Carol said she's forgiven me for what happened and has given me her blessing to write this post but that's it. This blog will still be here, as a memorial to Henry but this will be the last entry. Then we phoned the police. I don't think Jake will be arrested for murder but they might get him for manslaughter and possession of a controlled substance.

Henry's house was almost empty. Carol was moving out to live closer to her family. I asked if I could look at Henry's room because I'd never been there before. I'd always seen a snippet through the window. All that remains now is a bed frame. Even the light shade had been taken away. It was like I'd completed a jigsaw puzzle only to find that there wasn't a picture. I looked out of the windows, the blinds and curtains gone, at my own house. You can't see the moss or damp from this side and I've left the light on in my room. My curtains seem to glow and beneath the empty night sky it was the only source of light.

I hate empty houses. It's like the people who used to live there didn't exist. They are the forgotten. Yeah, they mattered to someone at some point but not to the world at large and no one will know about them. No one will remember the life of Henry Andrews.

But I will.

I hope you will too.